MIRROR, MIRROR

VIRGINIA NIELSEN

SCHOLASTIC INC.
New York Toronto London Auckland Sydney

Photograph by Owen Brown

ISBN 0-590-41066-0

12 11 10 9 8 7 6 5 4 3 2 1   7 8 9/8 01 2/9

Printed in the U.S.A.   01

Mirror, Mirror

A Windswept® Book

WINDSWEPT TITLES
FROM SCHOLASTIC

Don't Walk Alone by Mary Bringle
Someone Is Out There by Carole Standish
Girl in the Shadows by Miriam Lynch
The House of Three Sisters
   by Virginia Nielsen
Yesterday's Girl by Madeline Sunshine
The Snow's Secret by Carole Standish
The Red Room by Kaye Dobkin
The Silvery Past by Candice Ransom
Dreams and Memories by Lavinia Harris
A Forgotten Girl by Elisabeth Ogilvie
The Ghost of Graydon Place
   by Dorothy Francis
The Silent Witness by Meredith Hill
The Empty Attic by Jean Francis Webb
Murder by Moonlight by Dorothy Woolfolk
The Girl Cried Murder by Dorothy Woolfolk
House of Fear by Willo Davis Roberts
Mirror, Mirror by Virginia Nielsen

CHAPTER

ONE

I stood at the living room window and watched her come up the walk, shivers of excitement running up my back. It was uncanny how much she was like me. It was like walking toward a mirror and then, when you stopped, seeing your reflection still walking toward you. Enough to give you goose bumps.

She was my twin — and until yesterday I had not known she existed.

There were two others with her — a lean redheaded man and his tall wife, whom I immediately resented. The girl was wearing a pinkish plaid shirt and a white skirt. Inside the house, I glanced down at my own pink camisole and white shorts. Her hair was the same sandy blond color as mine — "Gilly vanilla," Ryan calls it — and it fell in the same long, loose waves.

What made her choose that style? It doesn't just happen, I knew. I knew to the

1

minute how much time it had taken her to blow-dry her hair for that effect.

The doorbell rang. I ran to the door and flung it open, and we were face to face.

"Hello," I breathed. "I'm Gillian . . . I guess I didn't have to say that, did I?"

"No." Her smile was mine, yet strangely different. "And I don't have to tell you I am Geraldine. But please call me Gerry." She even had my voice, sounding eerily like a rcording I had made at school.

"You can call me Gilly."

"Gilly," she said, as if tasting it. She nodded, smiling that mysterious smile.

Then my mother was behind me, inviting everyone in, and my father was shaking hands awkwardly with the redheaded man. Gerry and I examined each other with a wary interest.

Funny. Every time I felt misunderstood I used to daydream about being an adopted child. The reality of yesterday's revelation was something very different. My mother had brought out an old photograph album I had never seen before, and I had looked with disbelief at the snapshot of the laughing young woman she said was her younger sister. She told me, "Her husband was killed in a hunting accident, and two months later, she died after giving birth to identical twin girls. You came to us, Gilly, but your Uncle Justin took your twin to raise."

"You — you're not my real mother?" I was stammering, my tongue suddenly paralyzed.

She looked hurt. "Gilly, dear, what is a real mother? My sister carried you for nine months, but I've mothered you for all of your sixteen years!" Her hand moved across the page and I realized belatedly that the two near-naked babies propped up in an over-stuffed chair must be a picture of me and my twin.

"We would have taken both of you," she said, wistfully. "After all, Justin had Rob. But he wanted a little girl, too."

I felt no kinship to the woman in the snapshot. How could I? But there was churning in my stomach when I looked at the two babies.

"You didn't tell me!" It seemed monstrous that I hadn't know about the other one. I had been deceived — and by the two people closest to me.

"We planned to tell you about your mother when you were old enough to understand —"

"But you didn't tell me I had a *sister!*"

There had been a time when I longed for a sister to sleep with me and giggle with me. Although I was excited by the discovery I had a twin, I was apprehensive, too. For sixteen years I had thought of myself as unique. And she was just like me? It was a thought I found vaguely threatening.

"It's a long story," my mother sighed. She was nervous, telling me. She kept twisting the rings on her ring finger as she talked, her usually cheerful face sober under the untidy red hair.

"We cheated you and Geraldine out of

growing up together, Gilly. We didn't intend to. When you were babies we brought you together often. We even talked about letting you dress alike when you were older, if you wanted. I thought — I suppose I imagined having you both from time to time as you visited back and forth. But I never got on well with Justin's wife, and we had a big row and—" She gave a helpless shrug. "Well, we've patched it up now, and we've agreed that you and Geraldine should have an opportunity to meet. If it isn't too late, Gilly, dear. They're coming tomorrow. I haven't seen them for fifteen years."

Now we were together in the living room, all six of us. There was my Uncle Justin Partridge and his fashionably slender wife, Kara, in a cream silk dress. Facing them were the only parents I had known, looking slightly ill at ease beside those other two. *And my twin.*

The Partridges had driven a hundred miles. My father — I can't think of him as anything else — was trying to help with small talk about weather and crops. But the atmosphere was heavy with that old quarrel and the things that were not being said.

Our town was a small market town in the agricultural San Joaquin Valley. The Partridges were from the city. They had lived in San Francisco for fifteen years. The four of them were straining to find a common ground.

Strangely, I knew exactly how Gerry was

feeling. That was the exciting thing, how quickly I knew what she was thinking.

She was as apprehensive as I was, yet oddly exhilarated by an unexpected sense of freedom. Neither of us had parents. Instead, we shared four aunts and uncles. But we had something that had been missing before: We had each other.

I looked at my twin, intensely curious about her. "Come up to my room," I invited her, impulsively. "We can talk there."

"Yes, Gilly." There was relief in my mother's tone. "You girls go on, now, and get acquainted." She smiled nervously at Aunt Kara, who nodded her agreement.

I took Gerry up the stairs and into my room overlooking the orchard. She walked all around, touching things, and paused to look out of the window.

Finally I had to break the silence. "The cherries are gone," I said. "The peaches and pears are still green."

Gerry didn't answer.

That was dumb, I thought. She could see the fruit was green. And who cared?

She walked to the mirror, and I followed her. It was an old cheval glass, and I tilted it so we could see ourselves full-length.

"That's neat!" Gerry said.

"My mother's crazy about antiques — she goes to all the old farms and pokes in attics —"

"You mean your Aunt Judy." The way she said it spoke volumes. It startled me, too, made me think of Mom as a woman named Judy who had taken her dead sister's child to raise.

Gerry in the mirror was more like me than Gerry in the flesh. It was like a double reflection. We were the same height, we parted our hair on the same side, the dark lashes shading her hazel eyes were as long as mine. Our smiles now looked identical.

She spoke into the mirror. "I can never call my aunt 'Mother' again. Imagine never telling us, all this time!"

"Why tell us now?"

"Don't you know? We're going to Europe this fall, and I have to get a passport. My birth certificate says my name is Geraldine Amory, a twin. They had to tell me why I'm not Geraldine Partridge." She looked at my stunned face. "Didn't they tell you your real name is Amory?"

"I hadn't thought to ask. It's been too — I just can't take it in."

"Yeah."

"I wonder why they didn't adopt us?"

"The courts probably wouldn't have let them separate us."

My resentment grew. For sixteen years my parents had let me think I was an only child. I'd still think that now if the Partridges had not wanted to go to Europe. Mom had put all the blame on Uncle Justin, but I'd noticed she was the one who couldn't get along with Aunt Kara.

Neither of us suggested it, but in silent agreement Gerry and I kicked off our shoes

6

and sat cross-legged on the bed. Again we studied each other.

"We are very alike, aren't we?" Gerry said, finally. "But we're not mirror twins."

I was not sure what she meant, so I said, "In the mirror you looked more familiar somehow."

"Because our reflections were the same. Looking at each other we're seeing ourselves as others see us. Not very many people can manage that." She paused, studying me. "I should think it would make it harder for people to tell us apart."

Yes, that was it, I thought. In the mirror her reflection, like mine, was reversed. I was used to seeing mine reversed. That was why her smile, so familiar in the mirror, was different again. We stared at each other, intrigued.

After a while Gerry said, "Have you sometimes had a crazy feeling that you weren't whole, that there was some part of you missing?"

"Like half a brain?" I cracked.

But she was serious as she said, "Just a weird sense of being incomplete."

I knew what she meant. The feeling had haunted me. Did we have some unconscious memory of that time when we'd shared a womb? Had we been two halves of the same seed? Was there still some intangible tie between us?

We looked at each other, and I saw that she knew what I was thinking. It was a bit frightening to be able to slip into her mind;

7

even more, to see Gerry slipping into mine, too.

"Do you have a boyfriend?"

"Yes." I drew a deep breath as I wondered if Ryan would see any difference in us. I wanted desperately for him to be able to tell me from Gerry. "His name is Ryan Andrews," I told her. "He's a senior."

"I'm going with Mark Dolan." She jumped up, found her purse where she had thrown it on a chair, and dug out a snapshot. It was a picture of a good-looking guy in a football uniform, holding his helmet.

I could see that he was attractive, but I didn't think he was as handsome as my Ryan. While I looked at Mark, Gerry went to my dresser and examined the snaps I had stuck in my mirror frame. "Is this Ryan?"

It was a color shot I had taken when we were canoeing at the lake. He was in bathing shorts and he was clowning, holding up the oar as if threatening the camera. His brown hair was windblown, and his eyes were crinkled with laughter. I loved that picture because it reminded me of an absolutely perfect day, but it probably didn't do Ryan justice. Gerry only said, "Ummm."

The telephone rang, and I let it ring twice before I picked it up. It was quiet downstairs, and we could hear my mother say, "Gilly's got it. It's probably for her, anyway."

"I've got my own line," Gerry murmured.

"Oh, hi, Ryan," I said into the phone, feeling the flush of pleasure that always came when he called. Gerry got up and left the room, but then I heard a soft click and realized she had found the extension in my parents' bedroom.

"Whatcha doing?" It was his standard opening, but the way he said it made you feel he really wanted to know.

"Nothing," said Gerry on the extension, and she sounded like me.

"Want to go to a movie?"

"I don't know, we've got company —" I began, and Gerry finished "— but I could get away long enough to meet you for a hamburger."

"Well . . ." He sounded surprised. I giggled, expecting him to say, "Hey, what is this? Who's on the line?"

But he didn't. So I teased, "Unless you want to look for another date for the movie?"

"Heck, no, Gilly."

"Where shall I meet you?" Gerry demanded, and I drew in my breath.

"How about the Roost?"

"Fine," I said. I wanted Gerry to meet him, anyway. Didn't I? "Half an hour?"

"Okay."

Gerry ran back into my room and collapsed on the bed. "He never guessed there were two of us on the line," she laughed.

And it had been so easy! A little too easy, something was telling me. But wasn't this part of being a twin? I quickly squelched my doubts.

9

"You know, I don't think our aunts and uncles could tell us apart," Gerry said.

"My folks could," I said, confidently.

"Your folks?" she mocked.

"My parents," I said, deliberately stubborn.

This time she just lifted an eyebrow. I was beginning to churn inside again. When she said, "Let's test them," I had to say, "Why not?" There was no way my mom and dad would mistake Gerry for me!

Quickly, we changed clothes. I put on the plaid shirt and the pretty flared skirt. They fit perfectly but felt strange, scented with a perfume that was not my own.

Now when we stood side by side before the mirror I was confused. There I was, looking exactly like the girl I had seen coming up the walk an hour ago. And there beside my image stood another self, wearing the clothes I had put on when I got up that morning.

I had the illusion that I was standing outside my body, watching myself. The thought came to me that this must be the way a person feels when she dies, and I shivered.

"Somebody walk over your grave?" Gerry asked, lightly.

"Gerry, don't say that!"

"Come on." She caught my arm, and we ran down the stairs together.

They were still in the living room, relaxing over drinks. The atmosphere had warmed up a little. A tray of cheese and crackers sat on the coffee table, and Gerry and I helped ourselves.

"There are cold Cokes in the refrigerator for you and Gerry, honey," my mother said. *She was speaking to Gerry!*

"Okay," Gerry said, and while I stood there, stunned, my twin sister went into the kitchen as naturally as if she had lived here all her life. I couldn't believe it was really happening.

"Are you and Gilly getting acquainted?" Aunt Kara asked me. Her nails were long and glossy and her makeup was perfect. My mother wasn't wearing any makeup and there was a faint shine to her skin, but I knew she didn't care. I thought I understood why they had not "got on."

When I still had not found my tongue, Aunt Kara turned to my mother and said in an amused tone, "Have you noticed they are both wearing pink and white?"

Neither of them, I thought, bristling, could see beyond a pink plaid shirt.

Everyone hears stories about twins fooling their friends and teachers, and it sounds like such fun. But nobody talks about the hurt when the people closest to you can't tell you apart. I had lost my identity. I had thought I was a person, but I was half of something known as twins. Who knew which half? And who cared?

When Gerry came back with the Cokes, my mother said, "Why don't you take them out on the patio, dear. We've still some catching up to do, and I know you two have better things to talk about."

"Right," Gerry said, with a peculiar emphasis.

"What did I tell you?" she said, grimly, when we were out of earshot. "They haven't the foggiest who's who."

"Real parents could tell," I said with the bitterness of my betrayal.

That was how it began, that terrible time I won't ever forget. Looking back, I can't lay all the blame on Gerry, for out of my hurt I fell in with her suggestion that we exchange places. But it *was* Gerry who suggested it. It was a long time before I knew why.

CHAPTER

TWO

The Partridges invited me to return with them to San Francisco for a week's visit.

"I like your Ryan," Gerry told me, as we rode toward the coast in the backseat of Uncle Justin's car Sunday evening.

I wasn't surprised. But I was disappointed in Ryan. He said it had blown his mind, seeing two of us, and he was full of sarcastic remarks about our doubling his fun. It didn't bother him at all when he failed to tell us apart. Gerry thought it was great, but I felt let down.

"You'll like Mark, too. He's really neat."

I wondered what Mark would be like. A snapshot doesn't really tell you much.

Ahead of us in the front seat of the luxurious little foreign car, Aunt Kara played classical music on the tape deck and gossiped with Uncle Justin about their San Francisco friends, not paying us the slightest attention. I didn't know if she was being tactful, or if she was bored by our nonstop chatter. Although Gerry and I had talked all day and half the night comparing notes on our lives during the time we had been separated, we still hadn't run out.

Gerry was asking lots of questions, so she must have been as curious about my life in the ranch-style house in the valley as I was about her life in San Francisco. Or so I thought.

Aunt Kara was very different from my mother. She rode with her head tilted and her chin lifted like a fashion model, looking very aristocratic, but I thought the perfection of her profile was rather cold.

The sun was sinking over the hills of the coast by the time we reached the last pass, and when the city came into view, her fabulous towers were glowing with colors softened by a gauzy fog. Through it, the lights marking the two bridges gleamed like strings of pearls.

The odors carried on the moist sea air were salty and faintly fishy, with a hint of roasting coffee. It was all very different from the dry valley air that smells of dusty vineyards and mown hay and fertilizer. It was impossible not to wonder what my life would be like if I had been the twin adopted by Uncle Justin and the house on the bay side of Russian Hill had always been my home.

The house was tall and extremely narrow, closely hugged by its neighbors. A half-dozen steps rose directly from the sidewalk, which was separated from the two postage-stamp patches of grass by a retaining wall topped by a wrought-iron fence. The house was painted a fresh gray with all its curlicue decorations white, and its front door was a bright turquoise with a shining brass knocker in the shape of an anchor.

Gerry's bedroom was on the top floor. It was cool and elegant, with low twin beds under pale beige spreads and clean-lined Danish chests. But her window looked down on gaudy Fisherman's Wharf, with its restaurants ablaze with neon signs, and on the small forest of fishing craft masts beyond it. At the far end of Restaurant Row, an old four-masted sailing schooner was silhouetted against the shiny waters of the dark bay.

"The *Balclutha*," Gerry said. "A floating museum."

I stared, entranced.

Gerry drew the drapes and turned on a light between the beds. I looked around the room, thinking it austere. There was scarcely an accent of color among its neutral tones of beige and tan and gray.

As usual, Gerry read my mind. "There is so much color out there," she explained, gesturing toward the draped window.

"Can we open the drapes again when we're ready for bed?"

"I always do."

Down the hall I could hear Aunt Kara's high voice on the telephone. We hurried into our pajamas, leaving our unpacking until morning, then turned off the lights and lay against our pillows, looking out at San Francisco Bay. The garish lights of the wharf were transmuted by the mist into lovely pastels. It had an aura of romance and adventure that made my own orchard view seem commonplace. I wondered resentfully why Uncle Justin couldn't have adopted us both.

"It must be nice to be an only child."

I looked at Gerry in surprise. "I think it would be great to have an older brother."

She shrugged. "It's not that great. When I was little Rob teased me unmercifully. Now he ignores me. And he gets the best of everything."

I reflected on that. *The view from the other side of the valley,* my father was fond of saying. *It's not necessarily better, it's just different.*

Gerry continued, "Of course, Rob's seldom home since he started college. This summer he's working for the forest service."

Lights bobbed on the masts of the fishing craft in the basin beyond the wharf. Some of them were already moving out into the bay. Beyond them was a dark mass Gerry said was Alcatraz, the ill-famed island prison of long ago.

"The boats will come back in at daybreak. If we wake up early we'll go down to the wharf and see them unload their catch."

"I won't sleep a wink! I couldn't close my eyes on that view."

The telephone between the beds rang — Gerry's private line. "It's Mark," Gerry said. "You answer it."

"Oh, no!"

16

"Just pick it up and say hello," she urged, "and see what happens."

The phone rang again. I looked at her.

"I really want to know, Gilly."

I picked up the phone and said, "Hello?"

"Hello, pork pie," said a deep, warm voice like I'd never heard except in my dreams.

"*Pork pie?*" I exploded, and heard Gerry suppress a giggle. "That's a crazy name to give a girl."

"I'm glad you like it." He laughed, and a little ripple of excitement traveled down my body, all the way to my toes. At the same time something said quite clearly in my head, *He's someone I'm afraid to meet.*

Silently I handed the phone to Gerry, and tried not to listen as she cooed into it, telling him about her weekend with me. Of course, I heard every word.

"He's coming over tomorrow night," she told me, after she hung up. "He wants to meet you."

It was more than the view that kept me awake that first night in San Francisco. Gerry fell into a deep sleep but I was not even drowsy. Over and over my mind played back that amused *Hello, pork pie,* as I tried to fit the voice to my memory of the snapshot Gerry had shown me.

After a while I became aware that outside the window the fog had deepened until the lights down on the wharf were dim. The bay was hidden. Traffic along the bay highway had ceased except for an occasional car I could see but not hear, moving on some mysterious errand along the waterfront, its lights illuminating shadowy buildings and creepy alleys.

Then the foghorns began their eerie sounds. One groaned as if in deep pain; another wailed as if grief-stricken; once or twice I heard one that seemed a faint, faraway shriek of terror.

It must have been the foghorns that made my sleep fitful, broken by nightmarish dreams in which I was being chased by some unimaginable danger, experiencing all the pain and grief and terror the sounds seemed to express.

"How can you sleep through those awful groans?" I asked Gerry in the morning.

She laughed. "In three nights you won't even hear them."

I doubted that.

After breakfast she showed me the rest of the house, a renovated San Francisco Victorian, she called it. Off the entry was a large dining room, and behind it the kitchen and a very pleasant smaller room, overlooking a tiny rear garden, where Gerry and I breakfasted alone. Uncle Justin had long ago gone to his office, after taking coffee up to Aunt Kara in the master bedroom.

"I'm the only one who uses this room since Rob left," my twin told me. "Justin has breakfast downtown and Kara just has coffee."

I had never in my life eaten breakfast alone. "You don't mind?"

"No. We value our privacy around here."

I wasn't sure whether she was being ironic or just matter-of-fact.

On the second floor there was a large living room, spare and elegant in the same way Gerry's bedroom was, all cool neutral colors with few accents. Its windows also faced the bay, which was its chief decoration. This was apparently Aunt Kara's style.

Behind the living room was Uncle Justin's study and a small sitting room that doubled as guest quarters, sharing a bath with Rob's room. On the top floor were Gerry's room and the master bedroom, each with its private bath.

"Well, how do you like it?" Gerry asked me.

"It's beautiful — like a mock-up in a decorating store."

"Exactly." She grimaced. "Your house is more comfortable, isn't it? It must be fun living in a small town."

"It's not as exciting as this." But exciting in a rather intimidating way. I didn't say that, but I didn't have to — Gerry knew how I felt.

We were sitting cross-legged on her bed, just as we had sat on mine, still exploring our likes and differences, still amazed at how many times we had made the same choices — we both love artichokes, for instance, and

19

can't stand those fancy little chicken potpies; we both signed up for Spanish as an elective.

"Do you play tennis?"

"I was very big on tennis when I was fourteen," I admitted.

"So was I!" Gerry exclaimed. "I played every Saturday morning. You have to get up at dawn around here to get a court, and I didn't have an alarm clock. So my girl friend would come by and yank on my string —"

"Your *what?*"

"Yeah. I tossed one end out of my window and hung it over the fence. When I went to bed I tied the other end around my big toe —"

"Gerry, you didn't!"

"Justin took a dim view of anybody ringing the doorbell that early," she said gloomily. "One night I'd hardly got to sleep when someone yanked on the string. It was one o'clock in the morning! Can you imagine?" she asked, indignantly. "Some stranger walking by yanked my string!"

I fell back on the bed, laughing. "I don't see how anyone could resist yanking it. I couldn't."

Aunt Kara came by our door, dressed for a luncheon. "I thought you were going to take Gilly to the wharf this morning?"

"We got up too late. Maybe tomorrow," Gerry said, carelessly, and Aunt Kara went on, satisfied.

We spent the afternoon going through Gerry's closet, which was filled with beautiful clothes, some of them more sophisticated than my mother would let me buy. Gerry claimed she hated them all and preferred her jeans, but Aunt Kara would not let her come to dinner in them.

So that fateful night, which I look back on now as the beginning of all that happened, I was wearing one of my prettiest dresses. We came downstairs together. The door of Uncle Justin's study was open and I saw he had a visitor.

I had just glimpsed the well-dressed man who sat with his back to the door when Gerry said, behind me, "You go on down to the kitchen and see if you can help Kara get dinner on." She had solved the problem of what to call her parents by using first names. "I've forgotten something."

She turned and ran quietly back upstairs.

Wondering what she could have forgotten that was so important, I went on downstairs. I found no one in the kitchen, but almost immediately the side door, which was the service entrance, opened and Mark Dolan came in.

He was older and more mature than I had imagined from his snapshot; he made Ryan seem like a boy. That was my first impression — that and his surprising height and the impact of his golden brown eyes, glowing with vitality — and then the most extraordinary thing happened. I found myself clasped tightly in his arms, and he was kissing me!

I was pressed against his woolly sweater. The shock of his lips, firmly demanding yet velvety soft against mine, sent a quiver through me.

He let me go at the same time that I heard the quick footsteps behind me. Gerry said, "Hi, Mark. I see you've already met Gilly."

"My God!" Mark said, over my head. "I don't believe it!"

Gerry laughed, and I wondered at the tone of triumph in her laugh. Hadn't she seen Mark kissing me? Or didn't she care?

I felt heat rising to my face, and Mark's quick apology did not help. I could not meet his eyes and was grateful for Aunt Kara's entrance into the kitchen at that moment.

"Gilly, dear, will you set the table while Gerry and I do the gravy and the biscuits? Mark, are you staying for dinner?"

"No, thank you. I stopped by to see Gerry and —"

"Gilly," Gerry finished for him.

His warm, interested gaze rested on me. He was smiling.

"How many places, then, Aunt Kara?" I asked, hastily. "Is the gentleman with Uncle Justin staying?"

Her eyebrows went up. "Is Herb Pound still upstairs?"

"Yes," Gerry said.

"He won't be staying, he has a dinner date. I am so glad he is beginning to go out again."

"I saw him at the St. Francis with a nice-looking woman last week," Mark said.

"You did?" Aunt Kara stopped with a spatula in her hand to look at him. "I wonder if she was the one I saw him with?"

Mark shrugged, smiling.

"Herb lost his wife in a tragic accident," she told me.

"What happened?"

There was dead silence for a moment. Then Aunt Kara said, "Gerry didn't tell you?"

I shook my head. Gerry was standing a little apart. She had said nothing. Whatever happened seemed to have really disturbed her.

"She was shot with a high-powered rifle," Aunt Kara said flatly. "They were out on the bay in Herb's boat. The police said someone must have been firing at a sea gull. Herb was standing so close her blood spattered him —"

"Moth-er!" Gerry was pale, so upset she forgot to call her Kara.

"She was my best friend." I was surprised to see a glitter of tears in Aunt Kara's usually cool eyes before she turned away. "Since it's just the family, Gilly, use the dishes and silver in the little breakfront. You'll find some place mats there, too."

As I escaped into the hall, the man she had called Herb was running lightly down the stairs. He was about the age of my uncle, still handsome, and he had the look of a rich man with thick, professionally groomed hair, like the newsmen on television. There were muscles beneath his well-fitting suit.

"Gerry," he said in a hard voice, and went on through the entrance and out the front door before I could tell him I was Gilly.

I am not sure I would have told him. There

had been something in his closed face that froze me. Was it grief? I would ask Gerry to tell me more about that tragic accident, I decided. But something happened that night that drove the incident from my mind.

Again I was lying awake after Gerry had gone to sleep, my brain alive with the impressions of the day but returning too often to that surprising moment in Mark Dolan's arms, recreating my response to the touch of his lips.

The phone between our beds rang. Across the room the digital clock on the Danish dresser read 1:55. Gerry did not stir. I didn't want to pick the phone up, but I couldn't let it ring until it wakened not only Gerry, but Aunt Kara and Uncle Justin, too.

"Hello?" I said, softly.

There was someone on the line. I could hear breathing. Not loud, not rapid. Just someone out there breathing and listening. Outside the quiet room, down on the bay, the foghorns' gloomy wails were mingling. I couldn't make myself hang up. What if something terrible had happened at home?

Then I reminded myself this was Gerry's private line, and my father would call Uncle Justin if something were wrong. Could it be Mark? "Hello?" I said again, a little more loudly, hoping Gerry would wake up.

"Vengeance is swift and terrible."

At first I could not believe I had heard the incredible words. It was a disembodied voice — I could not tell whether it was a man's or a woman's, but it sent shivers through me.

"Who is this?" I cried.

But the line had gone dead. It was just a voice out of the fog, a troubled voice with a troubling message.

Gerry said, sleepily, "Who was it?"

"Nobody. I mean, I don't know." I told her what the voice had said.

She was silent so long I thought she had dropped off to sleep again.

"Gerry?"

"A nut," she mumbled. "We get that kind of call once in a while."

"But it sounded so — so threatening." I couldn't dismiss it so easily.

She raised herself and picked up her pillow, punching it flat. "You're in the city now, Gilly," she said, with a touch of impatience. "Things happen here, things a lot worse than a nutty phone call."

I wondered if she was thinking of the accident that happened to Herb Pound's wife.

"Forget it." She flopped down with her face turned away from me as if that disposed of the incident, but I had heard the tremor in her voice. She was more shaken than she wanted me to know.

CHAPTER

THREE

The next morning we got up at dawn, put on jeans and warm sweaters and raced down the steep sidewalks to the wharf. It was still foggy but in the gray morning light the fog was not threatening. The air carried a chill damp breeze off the ocean that I found exhilarating, and the day beckoned with a promise of exciting adventure.

The fancy restaurants were closed, but on the wooden piers behind those cafés on the waterfront, there was bustling activity. Fishing smacks were moored all along the piers and swarthy fishermen, laughing and shouting to one another, were unloading their slippery catches, which gleamed like silver coins spilling from an open sack.

On another pier a curly-haired young man was singing an operatic aria as he worked, his rich baritone mellowed by the heavy air between us. The just-risen sun was trying vainly to shine through the fog. Over our heads the sky was filled with screaming white gulls.

"Two, by gawd!"

I looked over my shoulder and saw a fisherman standing knee-deep in his catch in a dirty white tub with blue trim. Facing him on the pier was a dark-skinned man with bare muscular arms, whose head and most of his face were covered with black curly hair. Both were staring at us, and I didn't know which one had spoken. The exclamation had caught the attention of other young fishermen. They began whistling and calling, *"Bellissima, bellissima!"*

We giggled, enjoying the attention. It was the price — or depending on how you looked at it, one of the perks — of being a twin. But I felt uneasy, for some reason. It was hard to read the bearded man's expression through all that hair, but the eyes under the heavy black brows did not look as if they were saying bellissima. It seemed to me they were unfriendly.

When we tired of examining the fish we went through a walkway to the street and followed the fragrance of fresh coffee to a diner. We crowded in among the fishermen and early workers for coffee and doughnuts, and none had ever tasted better.

"Kara wants me to buy some shrimp," Gerry said, and she dragged me along the walk until we came to several great vats standing at the curb under an awning. Steam rose from them, carrying a rich aroma of cooking seafood. Behind the last vat stood a portly Italian wearing a long white apron and a spotless cap on his curly, graying hair. His teeth gleamed in a welcoming smile.

"Ah, Missa Gerry! How many shrimp this morning?"

"Hello, Joe. Give me three pounds."

He looked past her and his eyes widened on me. "You no tell me you have sister," he exclaimed, as he poured gray, fresh shrimp into the steaming vat.

"This is Gilly. She's visiting."

"Ah! She is cousin, then? As like as two ripe peaches!"

"Why not? We're twins."

"Ah!" Joe shook his head. "You're too young to marry," he reproached me.

I laughed. "I think so, too. I'm not married."

"You tease an old man," he complained. He pointed his ladle at me. "Are you twin, or no?"

"Yes."

He shook his head in bafflement.

Gerry laughed, but did not explain why her twin sister was only visiting. In the hot brine, the shrimp were slowly turning a delicate pink. In a few minutes Joe scooped them out with his long-handled strainer and wrapped them neatly in butcher paper. Gerry paid for them, said, "Come on," and darted into the street.

I followed her across and around a sharp corner to a bakery where she bought two long loaves of French bread that she handed

28

to me, and we started the long slow climb up the blocks we had raced down.

"Do you come down here often?"

"Yeah. Usually to pick up fresh fish or bread for Kara. I like to come early before the wharf is jammed with tourists. It's better in winter. There aren't such mobs everywhere."

"You come alone?" It seemed to me a hazardous thing to do, wandering the waterfront at dawn.

But Gerry said, "Why not? The fishermen are family men. Most of them live right around here." She added, casually, "Sometimes Mark comes with me, when we go sailing early. Have you ever sailed a Hobie Cat?"

"No, but I've seen one on the lake."

"A catamaran is the greatest. Maybe Mark will take you out while you're here."

My heart leaped. "Me? You mean both of us, don't you?"

"Yeah, well —" She gave me a speculative look. "He prefers sailing with only himself and one crew."

"Me? *Crew?*"

"It's not that difficult." She shrugged. "He'll probably take us both."

Why is it easier to climb a steep hill walking backward? I walked facing Gerry and looking beyond her to the waterfront. Already we were high enough to see over the buildings along the wharves. There were a dozen or so little triangular sails out on the water, which was turning blue as the sun burned off the mist. My imagination turned to Mark's sailboat, picturing myself with him out on that blue bay, and I felt a singing anticipation.

Later that morning Aunt Kara took us shopping. "Do you want dresses that are alike?" she asked us. "You're a little old for that sort of thing, but perhaps it's an experience you should have. What do you think, Gerry? Gilly?"

"Yes!" we cried, together.

The pleasure was in discovering that we wanted the same dress. There was no discussion about it; we spotted it at the same time and went straight to it. It was our dress, simple and elegant, a butter-yellow knit that gently hugged our figures and seemed to bring sparkles of sunlight to our eyes and hair. A dress that cried, *San Francisco!* We would have been crushed if the saleswoman had not had two in our size.

When we put them on, Aunt Kara said, only half-joking, "I'm not sure that was such a good idea. You will have to part your hair on opposite sides, or I'll be calling you both Gerrygilly."

Gerry tilted her head. "Not a bad name."

I shrugged. "Sounds like a county in Ireland."

"But a name we could both answer to."

"Yeah, save time and trouble."

We both laughed.

Oh, it was such fun having a twin!

I was shy and uncomfortable with Mark Dolan at first when he came to take us to the museums. We were to visit the DeYoung in Golden Gate Park first, have tea at the Japanese tea garden, then drive back to town and let Aunt Kara show us through the Museum of Modern Art, where she was a docent.

"A docent is a volunteer worker," she explained, for my benefit.

Every time I looked at Mark I remembered that stunning moment in his arms with his lips warm and firm on mine, and I blushed with embarrassment. I remembered how quickly he had dropped his arms when Gerry came into the kitchen, and I wanted to die.

I was so aware of him at my elbow, between me and Gerry, that the pictures we saw were a blur. The day was wonderful, and I loved the pretty little tea garden where we had tea and cakes, but I was relieved when it was over and Gerry and I were back in her room, squatting cross-legged on her bed and discussing Mark and Ryan. I was fascinated with every bit of information she dropped about Mark. He had two brothers, one older and one younger. His father was a great sportsman, had been a football hero when he was young. His mother was a friend of Aunt Kara's.

Gerry was insatiably curious about Ryan. How long had I known him? Were we in any classes together last year? What were his best and poorest subjects? Did we ever study together? How long had we been going steady? What about his family?

At dinner that evening Aunt Kara said,

"We must give a luncheon for Gilly so she can meet your friends."

"Oh, Kara!" Gerry's voice dripped with scorn. "Luncheons are so tiresome!"

I was hurt. "Yes," I said, quickly. "You needn't do that, Aunt Kara."

"A luncheon," Aunt Kara said, firmly, "introducing your newly found twin."

"I'll have to do it all," Gerry complained. "You'll be at the museum or someplace."

"You can wear your new dresses and confound everyone. It will be fun. How about Thursday?"

Gerry's reluctance was humiliating, but once it was settled, she entered into the spirit of the thing with zest. We planned the menu together and I checked off the names while she did the telephoning. On Thursday morning we dashed around Columbus Square picking up fruit and garlic olives and flowers for the table. At noon a dozen girls came, shrieking when they saw us standing side by side in our creamy knits, oohing and aahing and plying us with all sorts of questions.

After it was over, Gerry was oddly quiet. "I like your friends," I told her. "But meeting them all at once was a bit overpowering. I'll never remember all their names."

"Yeah," Gerry said, and added moodily, "I'd as soon have skipped it."

My hurt returned. "Why?"

She just shrugged. She was standing in front of her mirror and I went to stand beside her. There we were in our identical dresses, incredibly alike, and for the first time instead of marveling at our resemblance I was thinking sadly that she would always be a mystery to me — so like me and yet so different — and feeling a strange apprehension for the future.

"It's too late for us, isn't it, Gerry? We were kept apart too long."

Immediately her pensive mood shattered. "Don't say that, Gilly! Think how much fun we're going to have catching up! I want to know everything about you! Tell me what it's like living in an orchard."

We were wearing those dresses again on Saturday, after an exciting week of exploring the city with Mark as escort, when my folks drove up and parked at the steps of the narrow house. I don't know how Gerry managed to be the first one to throw her arms around my mother, exclaiming, "Aunt Judy!" Mom was wearing a hat, something she did so rarely that she looked strange to me. She was both admiring and slightly uncomfortable in Aunt Kara's austere living room.

"You'll stay for lunch?" Aunt Kara invited.

"Judy wants to visit some antique shops," my father said, with a look at us that said, *You know Judy!* "We'll catch lunch somewhere in between. Are you ready to leave, Gilly?"

"No," Gerry said. "Come on, let's finish packing."

"I'm all packed." I looked a question at Gerry.

My dad was shaking his head. "If you

hadn't spoken," he told me, in his slow-talking way, "I'd have thought you were Gerry."

Gerry laughed, and jerked her head toward the stairway. I knew she wanted a last word with me before I left. We ran up to the next floor together.

Breathless, she said, "Let me go in your place, Gilly, please!"

"Oh, no, we can't do that, Gerry! They'd know in a minute."

"You heard Uncle Garth. He can't tell the difference. Kara and Justin keep so busy they won't have time to look at you that closely."

"Dad said if I hadn't spoken," I reminded her. "Mom will surely guess."

"She didn't last week, did she? Please, Gilly. I want the experience of living in your house."

I understood very well what she wanted, and I longed to experience her life in the city, too. Switching places would enable us to learn intimate things about each other very quickly.

"Is it because of Ryan? You don't want me to go out with him?"

I shook my head. "No, I don't think I'd mind, really." If he couldn't tell us apart it made no difference.

"I think I could go for him," Gerry confessed. "Would that hurt you, Gilly?"

It was my turn to confess. "I think I already like Mark better."

Her eyebrows shot up and her laugh was

shaky. "At least we can find out this way, can't we?"

Uncle Justin came running up the stairs. "Is your luggage ready, Gilly?"

"Yes," Gerry said, before I could speak.

"Don't forget to call him Justin," she warned me, as he went back downstairs.

"Don't *you* forget to say Mom and Dad!" I retorted.

I turned to go but Gerry stopped me with a hand on my arm. "I almost forgot. You will be taking part in a bike-a-thon for the ASPCA Thursday. Kara's a director, or something."

"*Gerr-ee-ee!*" I wailed.

"You can ride a bike, can't you?"

"Of course, but —"

"No problem, then. There's a sheet on the bike-a-thon there in my desk. Anyway, Mark's got all the dope. You're going partners with him."

Would I have agreed if my heart had not tripped over itself every time I saw Mark that first week? At any rate, I am as much to blame as Gerry for what happened next.

I hung back when Uncle Justin carried my bags, and Gerry walked casually down the steps with Mom and Dad. She slid into the backseat of our old Buick. I stood with Kara and Justin on the stoop in my identical yellow knit dress, waving good-bye. It was the strangest feeling, watching the familiar car move down the street with Gerry in my backseat spot.

The house felt very different with her gone

— colder and more alien. There was little conversation at the dinner table. Naturally, I was quiet — I had no idea what to say! I studied my Uncle Justin and marveled at how Mom's brother could look so much like her, in a thin sort of way, and be so different in temperament. Mom was ordinarily relaxed and easygoing and laughed a lot; Uncle Justin was like redheaded people are supposed to be. He kept lining up his knife and his spoon with nervous fingers and he snapped at Aunt Kara when she brought the coffee in because he said it was cold, which infuriated her and made her damn their new coffee maker.

Maybe, I pondered, it was the person they were married to who made the difference. Aunt Kara was obviously a perfectionist, demanding of herself and others, while my dad moved and talked deliberately with little excitement but great good humor.

That night, alone in the beige bedroom with the private line, I discovered the view was not that fabulous when I was not sharing it.

Sometime later I awakened from sleep and picked up the ringing phone before I was really aware of what I was doing. When no one answered my mumbled "H'lo?" I quickly hung up, belatedly remembering that disembodied voice and its terrible warning.

Almost immediately the phone started ringing again. I pushed it down under the covers, but it kept ringing. Panicky now, I thought I heard noises of stirring in the master bedroom so I reached down and jerked the phone off its cradle.

After a moment I began hearing thin sounds from under the covers. "Gerry! Gerry! Are you awake?"

I snatched the phone up from under my blanket and breathed into it, "Mark?"

"Wow! Are you hard to wake up!" It was the deep warm voice that had said, *Hello, pork pie!* I imagined I could see those lively brown eyes. "Want to go sailing?"

"Is it morning?"

"That it is, my love, that it is."

My heart was beating wildly. "I'll be ready in fifteen minutes."

"Uh — don't forget to dress warmly. You know how cool that bay breeze can be." His tone had subtly changed and I wondered if I had been too eager.

"Right," I said, trying to sound like Gerry.

When I went downstairs Uncle Justin was making coffee. "You're up early," he said, smiling at me. He was dressed for the office in a vested gray suit, his bright hair brushed flat but still damp.

"I'm going sailing with Mark."

"Then you'll want a thermos of coffee to take with you." He opened a cupboard, took down a thermos jug, and filled it with hot water. "Have a good visit with your twin?"

"Yes." I was suddenly ashamed, wanting to blurt out that I was Gilly, in his kitchen under false pretenses. Darn Gerry, anyway!

Then he said, "Have you forgiven me?"

"What for?" I asked, warily.

"For separating you girls."

I didn't even have to wonder what Gerry would say. "No. I think it was a terrible thing to do."

His eyes, so like Mom's, reproached me, then he looked away. I was confused; I had told him the truth, and yet I felt guilty. He took down a pretty cup and saucer, poured coffee in it for Aunt Kara, and left for the upstairs master bedroom. "Have fun," he said, over his shoulder.

I had just emptied the thermos bottle and refilled it with coffee when Mark rapped on the kitchen door. I opened it with the thermos in my other hand, and Mark directed an appreciative glance at it as he asked, "Ready?"

He was wearing a dark pullover and above it his face was rosy from the cold wind. I found myself looking at the curve of his lips and remembering their softness, and I could feel my cheeks warming. He was checking my costume — tennis shoes, jeans, and sweater. "Don't forget your windbreaker."

"Is it that cold?"

"When the fog burns off we'll be shedding wraps, but take it."

At last we were in his little car, heading out toward the yacht harbor, west of Fisherman's Wharf and beyond Aquatic Park and Fort Mason. We left the car in the parking lot, and Mark led the way out on one of the painted piers, past rows of idle boats.

"That's Herb Pound's boat," he said, pointing out a cabin cruiser at a dock in a deeper basin. "I don't think he's taken it out since it happened."

I didn't have to ask what *it* was.

As I looked at the trim cruiser with the shining brasswork on its mahogany rail, *Black Tern* lettered on its white hull, I pictured the handsome, assured man I had seen in Aunt Kara's house holding his wife in his arms while her blood ran down to the deck. "It must have been terrible for him."

"Yeah, he was standing right beside her. He must still wonder if the shot was meant for him."

Surprised, I said, "I thought some creep was shooting at a gull?"

"Wouldn't *you* wonder?" Mark asked.

CHAPTER

FOUR

Already the sun was dancing on the water and brightening the light-colored apartment houses facing the marina, making the day look deceptively warm. The stiff breeze that was scattering the fog was cool, and I was glad Mark had warned me to bring a windbreaker. He did not have to remind me to leave my shoes in his car. I was trying desperately to remember all the other things I had learned when he had taken both Gerry and me out three days ago.

"It isn't a 'steering gizmo,'" he had said at one point, in exasperation. "It's a tiller!" Then he had complained, exaggeratedly, "It's bad enough to have one landlubber aboard who doesn't know the difference between a halyard and a bowline." Then he had laughed when Gerry said, indignantly, "I do too know the difference!"

The catamaran was already in the water, bobbing gently. I grasped a line and stepped down on the canvas deck stretched taut between its two slender hulls. Mark untied it and followed me. I knew enough now to realize how skilled he was as I watched him unfurl his sail and position it so that it caught enough breeze to let him maneuver his craft out of its slot and into the bay.

"Coil the bowline," he ordered me, "and stow it away."

"Aye, aye, sir!" I said, as smartly as Gerry had, and prayed my fingers would not be clumsy.

His sail was scarlet and at its triangular tip was the black logo: *DO4*. I had asked what it stood for the day the three of us had gone out.

"It's the *Dolan Four*," Mark told me. "Me, my father, and my two brothers."

"Move up nearer the bow," he ordered now from aft where he sat with the tiller, and I slid further away from him, sitting on the sidebar with my legs stretched out in front of me and my toes tucked under the hiking strap.

Out on the bay, with the sail humming as it caught the breeze, the catamaran moved with incredible speed. It was like riding a skateboard. The gulls following us out of the marina soon deserted us for a sedately moving yacht.

The magic of sailing on San Francisco Bay is that you get a gull's-eye view of the city and its two great bridges. Oceanward, the span arched colorfully across the Golden Gate to the hills of Sausalito and Marin County, toward which a white ferryboat was

41

making its lazy way. The bay was dotted with sails, many of them even more colorful than Mark's, some with three broad stripes of yellow and red and blue.

Running downwind, we passed by Fisherman's Wharf, seeing it as it must look to the fishermen coming home. Beyond the wharves rose the hills of the city, topped with shining towers. Mark's face was alive with exhilaration, and I knew I must be wearing a permanent grin. My jeans were damp with spray, but the sun was warm on my back and my bare feet. We had already shed our windbreakers, and Mark had stuffed them into the storage compartment in the hull.

We passed a docked three-masted schooner and I exclaimed, "That's the *Balclutha*, isn't it?"

"Yeah. Some difference, huh? It's over three hundred feet long."

Skimming by, we were no bigger than a raft below that towering black hull. Yet the *Balclutha*, too, had been propelled by nothing but the wind. Its sailors had lived aboard the vessel for months going around the Horn. I said, impulsively, "Can we go aboard her?"

Mark looked at me oddly. "You want to go the tourist route?"

I bit my lip, realizing Gerry must have been aboard the museum ship many times. Shrugging, I said, "It's been a while."

"I want to show you a sailing vessel that interests me more, right now. We're coming around."

Since I was not an experienced sailor, I did not immediately realize what he was telling me, and so was not expecting him to swing the boom around. I saw it coming out of the corner of my eye and, reacting instinctively, threw myself backward.

The next thing I knew, I was lying on my back with my head hanging over the water and my hair streaming in the wind, with only my toes, hooked under the hiking strap running down the center of the canvas, to hold me from sliding into the bay. The boom passed over me, and I jackknifed, praying the hiking strap would hold as I grasped the side bar and pulled myself up again.

Mark was sitting frozen, his face tense. "Sorry," he said, with obvious effort. "I should have warned you."

It had all happened too quickly to frighten me. Besides, I was wearing a life jacket, and I did not know then how numbingly cold the bay is. I did what I thought Gerry would have done. I laughed and slapped my head. "Pay attention, Gerry!"

Sprawled on the canvas deck, I listened to the luffing mainsail, sputtering in the wind like an outboard motor. Then Mark trimmed sail and we glided noiselessly around Angel Island and through the Tiburon Channel. At Sausalito, where the houses climbing the steep hill are almost buried in foliage, Mark tied up beside a strange-looking vessel lashed to a pier. Faded letters on its bow proclaimed it the *Sea Gypsy*. It was smaller than the

Balclutha, and it had no rigging and no masts. Its hull was greenish and its deck was stripped bare of superstructure. Workmen swarmed over it.

"Volunteers," Mark told me. "Sailors who come to watch an old salt restore the schooner, and stay to help him. That boat's around a hundred years old, so they've plenty to do. You'd be surprised if I told you the names of the Hollywood stars who've spent a weekend here scraping paint."

I guessed that Mark himself was one of the volunteers and I was in a quandary. Was I supposed to know about the project? He had brought me to see it so I thought it safe to say, "So *this* is the *Sea Gypsy.*"

As we watched the workmen digging for dry rot and fitting new timbers in place, Mark ticked off information about the old ruin. She would have two masts and a new superstructure. An old deepwater sailor was doing all the new rigging, all the shrouds and lines that would hold the masts in place. The more Mark talked the more his face glowed. I could see this meant something to him.

"The old-timers say she looked hopeless when McKeever bought her almost ten years ago. She had been tied up here since World War II, used as a cheap place to live. One guy even built a makeshift cabin on her deck."

"Where are your tools, Mark?"

We swung around to face the man who had spoken. It was Uncle Justin's friend, Mr. Pound, looking quite different, almost cheerful, in an open-necked sport shirt and a yachting cap. "Can you handle a chisel, Gerry?" he asked me.

"We're supervising today," Mark told him. "We thought we'd measure your progress against the *Balclutha*."

"That tub?" Mr. Pound scoffed.

"The *Balclutha* was restored by volunteers, too," Mark told me. "Volunteer money, that is. The labor unions did the work, and it only took them one year." He looked up at the *Sea Gypsy*. "She's coming along, isn't she?" We stood there admiring her graceful, sharpened bow.

"So you brought Gerry out to see her." Mr. Pound's eyes were a strangely flat shade of dark gray, hard to read, but his intensely personal look made me uncomfortable.

"I was telling her the experts told Mc-Keever not to waste his time and money," Mark said.

"That's right. But he put her in dry dock and discovered her hull was still good — it's sheathed in copper, as you can see."

"He's probably put into her every cent he's made for the last ten years."

"I wonder that his wife isn't insanely jealous, but she loves the old schooner, too. Well," Mr. Pound said, "I came to work, not to kibitz." He gave us a little half-salute and climbed the gangplank to her deck.

"He spoke quite naturally of the man's wife, didn't he?" I asked Mark, as we wandered back to the catamaran. "Is that a good sign?"

45

Mark shrugged. "This is probably good therapy for him." He untied and we cast off. As he tacked out into the bay, I looked back at the *Sea Gypsy*. Herb Pound was not working. He was leaning on the rail of the schooner, watching us.

This time I ducked when Mark swung the boom to catch the breeze, and we began skimming back toward San Francisco.

Never was there such a day. I thought I would never again enjoy canoeing after such scudding speed. We sailed until we heard the distant music of many church bells coming faintly across the water. Then we put in at the marina, and Mark bought us brunch at the yacht club.

On shore a strange reserve came over us. We ate in a silence I didn't know how to break. With Ryan small talk came easily, but it was all on the surface. I felt a strong urge to talk honestly with Mark, and I couldn't do that without giving myself away. I didn't understand the change that had come over him, and it worried me. Had I done something wrong, or was he wishing he were back with the men working on the *Sea Gypsy*? Maybe he was the moody type.

When we had finished eating, Mark said offhandedly, "Still want to go aboard the *Balclutha*?"

I jumped at the chance to spend another hour with him. "Oh, yes, Mark, let's!"

He gave me an unfathomable look and headed his car back toward Fisherman's

Wharf, where we joined a cluster of tourists waiting to go aboard the museum ship.

The ticket booth for the *Balclutha* stood beside a gate in a high wire fence. As I waited for Mark to buy the tickets I idly noticed the man standing in line just behind him. He looked very familiar. I thought I had seen him on the dock in Sausalito, but perhaps it was just that his luxuriant hair and beard made him look like so many other young fishermen of Italian extraction —

Fishermen! That was where I had seen him before — on the pier where the fishing boats unloaded their catches. Wasn't he the one who had exclaimed, "Two, by gawd!" amusing us so that first morning Gerry and I had gone down to the waterfront?

Apparently one of a kind was not noteworthy. He did not even look at me. Or perhaps I was wrong. There are so many beards.

The gangway was a rigid metal ladder, very steep, which rose from the asphalt-paved wharf. I climbed it gingerly, glad I was wearing tennis shoes.

Mark was very knowledgeable about old sailing vessels and made an excellent guide. The *Balclutha* had sailed around the Horn seventeen times, then it had carried lumber to Australia. For nearly thirty years it sailed between San Francisco and Alaska with a salmon cannery below its decks. Its last active life had been as a show ship sailing up and down the coast!

"She was used in that wonderful old movie,

Mutiny on the Bounty," Mark told me. "Ever see it? With Charles Laughton?"

I hadn't, but I made a mental note to watch for it.

Below deck now the *Balclutha* held old carved and painted figureheads of sailing vessels, most of them voluptuous women whose bodies flowed into the bow of the ship. On deck Mark pointed out the rigging, showing me how it would be installed on the *Sea Gypsy* when they had finished restoring its hull, and told me a blood-chilling story about a sailing vessel that had been shipwrecked off the Maine coast in colonial days.

"When it heeled over so far the water was washing over the deck, the surviving passengers and crew climbed the rigging to escape the waves. Even there the waves splashed icy water over them and when daylight came and a rescue boat put out to her, the passengers were frozen solid, still clinging to the rigging."

"Oh, Mark, what a horrible story!" We had just been through the master's quarters, and I was interested to learn the master's wife had sailed with him on the *Balclutha*'s last voyage, even taking along her sewing machine. I shivered, thinking of the storms and the loneliness that woman had braved to be with her husband. Somewhere in the back of my mind was a fantasy imagining Mark and me in their places.

After our sail it was easy to imagine Mark a sea captain. There had been a beguiling intimacy on the catamaran, a sort of partnership as I followed his instructions in handling the lines. I wondered if I had handled myself well, or if he had guessed I knew only what I had picked up last week watching Gerry.

When we came up on deck again and walked toward the gangway, there was a long line of tourists waiting to buy tickets and several people were on the twelve-foot ladder. A handful of visitors waited with us on deck to descend when the gangway was free. Someone behind me engaged Mark in conversation, but since I was first in line I stepped forward when the last climber reached the deck, and I put my foot down on the top step.

I don't know whether the ship moved against the wharf just then or whether someone lurched against me. At any rate I lost my balance. With a scream of terror I pitched forward, feeling my hand torn away from the rail I was clasping.

Luckily, just as I fell down the steps, a portly man came through the gate below me. He strode forward without looking up to see if anyone was descending, and he had his foot on the first step when I hit him. I knocked him to the pavement, but he broke my fall.

Mark was down in an instant bending over me. "Gilly!" he cried. "Gilly!"

And that's how I knew that he hadn't been deceived.

CHAPTER

FIVE

Mark was pale and shaken. "Are you all right? Gilly, are you hurt?"

I could move my hands and feet, but I was feeling very queer, lying on my back and staring up at the faces above me. Mark's was taut and strange. And he knew!

He helped me to my feet. The gentleman who had broken my fall was getting up. Apparently only his dignity was damaged. Someone handed him his glasses and he tried to brush the dust from his sleeves and his trousers.

Mark thanked him for saving me from a serious injury.

"I can't say it was my pleasure, miss," the man said, adjusting his glasses and trying to smooth his hair, "but I'm glad you're not hurt. Perhaps next time you won't be in such a hurry."

He was the one in a hurry! I thought. "Someone bumped into me just as I started down the ladder," I explained.

It hurt to put my weight on my right ankle, and I was limping a little as we walked to Mark's car. I was very conscious of the warmth of his hand holding my arm. The embarcadero was swarming with tourist pedestrians. Cars were moving very slowly through them. We sat in his car for several minutes, waiting for a break in the traffic.

Mark still looked shaken. "How long is this little game of yours going to go on?"

There was an edge to his voice and my heart sank. "Just until the next visit when we can switch places again." I looked at him anxiously. "You won't give us away?"

He sat for a moment staring through the windshield. Then he clenched his fist and, hitting it on the steering wheel, muttered, "Girls!"

Did he think we were trying to make a fool of him? I wished that I knew more about how things were between him and Gerry.

He seemed older now than he had on the Hobie Cat, with the wind tossing his hair about and his tanned face split in a grin. I didn't know whether he was angry or not, but he certainly wasn't pleased.

He ran his fingers through a lock of hair that had fallen over his forehead. I watched, admiring his profile but wishing he would smile. I didn't want him to be annoyed with me.

"I suppose Gerry is going out with your boyfriend? You *do* have a boyfriend at home, don't you?"

I nodded, feeling guilty. Gerry and I had

not stopped to think how our deception would make other people feel.

He saw an opening in the traffic and drove off, whipping me back against the seat. But in my dismay glowed a secret pleasure. Ryan had not seen any difference between me and my twin, but angry or not, Mark had. For some reason that made me glad.

We did not speak all the way up the hill to the narrow Victorian house. When Mark parked behind Uncle Justin's car beside the wrought-iron fence that protected the tiny patches of greenery, he turned to me. "What do you want to do while you are here, Gilly?"

The little knot of miserable guilt inside me melted like snow in the rain. "Oh, everything, Mark, everything! I want to know what it would have been like if my uncle had kept us together. And Gerry is learning how I live. That's why we're doing this. We've missed so much by not knowing we were twins."

The warmth came back into Mark's eyes then, and he said, "Okay, Gilly. Leave it to me."

"Beautiful!" I turned to smile at him, and the one he gave me in response — in his eyes as well as on his lips — was devastating. For a moment we were in accord, with something exciting and alive flowing between us. Of course, he could be doing this for Gerry, I warned myself, but I was suddenly happy. I grabbed the empty thermos and my windbreaker and let myself out of the car.

"I'll call you," Mark said.

"Okay." At the door I turned and waved, and he drove away.

It was a relief, having him know the truth. *I told Gerry we couldn't get away with it,* I thought, smugly. Aunt Kara must know, too, and Uncle Justin soon would.

But there was no indication that they suspected when I met them in the hall. They were dressed in the kind of casual summer clothes that were seldom warm enough for San Francisco, even in summer.

"Oh, there you are, Gerry," Aunt Kara said. "We're just leaving."

"Have a nice sail?" Uncle Justin asked, but his eyes had shifted to something else before I answered.

"Great!" I told him. "Where are you going?"

"Down the peninsula," Aunt Kara said, looking to see if she had everything she needed in her purse. "For brunch, with the Olivers. Is Mark coming back?"

"No."

"Why don't you call Sheilah?" She brushed my cheek with her lips. "The Olivers' number is on my pad if you need us."

Uncle Justin ruffled my already tousled hair in passing, and then they were gone. I stood in the hall, still holding the thermos and Gerry's windbreaker, feeling oddly let down. Suspect? They hadn't even looked at me.

Feeling lonely, I climbed the two flights to Gerry's bedroom. Sheilah was one of the girls Gerry had invited over for lunch to meet me. I remembered the name but not the face, and I had forgotten her last name.

By the time I reached the third floor, Gerry's private phone was ringing. I grabbed it. "Hello?"

"Hi." It was a girl's voice.

"Sheil?" I said, tentatively.

"Who else? Doing anything this afternoon?"

"No. Are you?"

"You don't have a date with Mark?"

"He took me sailing this morning."

"Oh. Want to come over?"

What a fool I was to let Gerry talk me into this! I knew I had met Sheilah, but I couldn't remember her face and I had no idea where she lived.

"I'm dying to hear more about your twin." She hadn't waited for an answer. "That's so fabulous, discovering her after all these years. And it's simply staggering how much alike you are. It knocks me out!"

"Yeah." I saw a way out of my dilemma. "I fell and twisted my ankle this morning. Why don't you come over here?"

I held my breath until she said, "Okay. See you."

When I opened the door at the clap of the brass knocker, I remembered her, a small girl with short dark hair and a pixieish face. She was carrying a record album. "Hi," she said: "Folks home?"

"No."

She nodded matter-of-factly and started up

the stairs. Obviously, she knew her way around. Probably better than I did.

In my room she put the record on the little stereo and sat down on the carpet in the lotus position. "Solved the big problem yet?"

How in the world had Gerry persuaded me this was going to be easy? I tried to bluff my way out by saying airily, "I have no big problems. Only little ones."

Sheilah looked at me for a minute, then said soberly, "Maybe it's smart to play dumb."

It was my turn to stare at her.

But she changed the subject. At least I thought it was changed. "What's new with Mark?"

"Oh, he was in good form," I said, warily. "We sailed over to Sausalito where they're restoring that old schooner. Mark's been working on it, you know."

She nodded, as if she did know. "You're so lucky," she said, her dark eyes wistful, "to have Mark to take you places."

"I know," I said, feeling wistful myself because I did not really have Mark.

"He's got everything," she sighed. "Looks, personality, smarts, a car —"

I laughed. None of that was as important to me as the times when Mark had smiled at me with genuine affection in his eyes, smiles that had seemed to bring us very close together.

Sheilah raised her hand to the crown of her head, curled her fingers in her short hair and twisted it up in a point, making her look more than ever like an elf. She was doing it so unconsciously I didn't dare laugh. "So tell me about your country twin," she said.

That was safe ground. I gave her a blow-by-blow account of our first day together, describing Ryan for her as I thought he had appeared to Gerry and telling her more than she wanted to know about my dad's orchards and our small town. It was surprisingly easy to put myself into Gerry's shoes, and a barrel of fun to describe my life-style through her eyes.

"Ever since you told me, I've been wondering what I would feel like if I discovered I had a twin," Sheilah said, thoughtfully. "I've been reading everything I could find about twins. You're identical mirror-twins, aren't you?"

"Identical, but not mirror. We don't look alike to each other, except when we look in the mirror." I repeated what Gerry had said to me. "That lets us see ourselves as others see us, not as we look to ourselves in the mirror."

"Which one is dominant, you or Gillian?"

"You've lost me, Sheil."

"They say one twin always leads, and the other follows. One usually makes the social contacts, initiates friendships for the pair — you know."

I thought about that. If one of us was dominant, it was probably Gerry. She seemed so sophisticated, so self-assured. And she certainly had initiated this switch of our identities.

"But we weren't together," I said aloud. "We've each had to make our own way."

"Yeah." Sheilah nodded, and said, matter-of-factly, "Maybe that's good."

I liked her, but she did not seem to see any difference between Gerry and me, perhaps because we talked only about things both Gerry and I were familiar with.

Before Sheil left, we made a date to have lunch downtown later in the week. Her visit had broken the long day, but after she left it was again lonely in the house. I sat in my bedroom looking out of my window and listening to records while the fog rolled in and gradually blotted out the lights across the bay.

When the garish wharf was muted to its misty nighttime pastels, I went to bed. Aunt Kara and Uncle Justin were still out. I pictured Gerry going to bed in my airy room with the windows open and the smells of the orchard drifting in, and wondered if Mom knew she was an impostor.

Aunt Kara seemed surprised to see me downstairs the next morning. Too late I remembered Gerry saying she usually breakfasted alone. Aunt Kara was in a rush; she had an early morning meeting at the Museum of Modern Art.

"I thought the museum was closed on Mondays," Uncle Justin said, spooning his grapefruit.

"That's why the docents are meeting today. It's a special training session. What are you doing today, Gerry?"

"Oh, some tennis, maybe," I improvised.

Aunt Kara looked startled, then her face cleared. "So that's why you're up early. I won't be home for lunch, dear. You can warm up that Brunswick stew —"

"I'll find something."

"Need some money, honey?" Uncle Justin asked.

I shook my head. It didn't seem right to take his money.

Aunt Kara left soon after he did, nylon legs flashing beneath her smart suit. Alone in the house I wandered around, wondering what to do. The leather appointment book Aunt Kara had left lying open beside the kitchen telephone caught my eye.

At home, Mom had a calendar pinned up on the wall and on it she wrote things she didn't want to forget, such as "Put out iris bulbs," "Plant radishes," or "Mrs. R. — take fresh bread."

Aunt Kara's month was crowded with teas and luncheons, with a party or a dinner almost every night. She and my uncle belonged to a wine-tasting club and a gourmet dinner club and to the Symphony Association, things like that.

I thought of how much Gerry must be left alone and wondered how she filled all the hours. I was sure she managed very well, but she was going to find it very different living with my folks!

The phone was ringing upstairs in my

room and I ran up to answer Gerry's private line. "Hi, Gerry! Surprise, I'm still in town." It was a girl's voice, strange to me.

"Who is this?"

"Tanya," she said reproachfully. "Want to meet me downtown this morning? I have to find a swimsuit before we leave for the lake."

"I guess so," I said, curious to see what this other friend of Gerry's was like. I couldn't remember her at the luncheon.

"Can you be at the St. Francis at ten-thirty?"

"Okay."

I caught the bus just down the slope and sat facing the sidewalk, watching the pedestrians and listening to the coarse hum of the traffic as it made its way back up and over the hill and down the other side. The sea air sweeping down the intersections was bracing even though the sun was shining, and I wondered if that was why the faces of the people walking looked lively and alert.

Tanya was a tall, willowy brunette with eyelashes so long I wondered if they were fake. I had never seen her before, but she walked up to me in the hotel lobby and said, "Hi, Gerry." It was another reminder that there were two of us exactly alike. How did I really feel about that?

Tanya had an exaggeratedly slow way of talking but she talked constantly, which made things easier for me. I listened and learned a little more about my twin — and Mark.

"You staying in town all summer?" Tanya inquired idly, as she pirouetted in the dressing room in a gorgeous blue-and-white-striped maillot. I wondered if she were trying to impress me with her modellike figure.

"As far as I know now."

"You're in luck. Mark's not going up to Tahoe this summer, either."

"How do you know that?"

She gave me a sleepy smile. "I have my sources."

I decided I didn't like her much. She probably would dance a jig if Mark asked her for a date. Or maybe he already had, I thought glumly, and bet myself that was why she was not invited to Gerry's luncheon. Mark hadn't called, as he had promised he would.

That evening Aunt Kara and Uncle Justin were out again, and I didn't move far from Gerry's private line, waiting for Mark's call.

It came very late, after I was in bed. I picked up the phone under my bedside lamp with no premonition. "Hello?" I said, picturing Mark with the phone at his ear, his warm brown eyes smiling at me.

But he didn't answer. There was a silence, nerve-wrackingly familiar.

"Hello!" I noticed that my voice had moved a key higher.

It was the same frightening, altered voice. This time it seemed to be quoting a Biblical passage.

"I will take heed to my ways, that I sin not with my tongue. I will keep my mouth with a bridle —"

The shock of it, after expecting to hear Mark's deep, velvety voice made me suddenly furious. I snapped, "Then do it, or I'll call the police!"

I slammed the phone down but my heart was beating hard, sending a rush of blood to my head. I raged at the person who could intrude on my privacy just by dialing a number, but more so at myself because I had been caught unawares and could not control the panic that was making me tremble.

The house seemed big and empty, and too quiet. And I knew that for the first time in several nights I would be unable to sleep through the weird and mysterious wailing of the foghorns.

CHAPTER

SIX

After a few minutes I picked up the telephone and tapped out my home number. When I heard her familiar cheerful hello, it was all I could do to keep from saying, "Mom?" I bit down on my lip, and then said, shakily, "Has — has Gilly gone to bed yet?"

"Oh, hello, Gerry! I'm sorry, but Gilly's out with Ryan. How are you, dear?"

"I'm — fine," I choked. "I — I just wanted to talk to — Gilly." I had almost said "you," it was so reassuring to hear her comfortable, easy voice.

"And Kara and Justin?"

"They're fine. They're out to dinner."

"I see. I'll tell Gilly to call you, okay?"

"Thank you, Aunt Judy," I said forlornly, and hung up.

Mom didn't know it was me. Gerry was out with Ryan, I didn't know where Mark was, and I was alone in the house with the Voice still repeating its weird message in my ears and the foghorns making their monotonous music below the hill. I wondered if the Voice would call again, and I shivered.

When I finally did go to sleep, the ringing of the telephone wakened me. Instantly my heart was banging against my ribs. I won't answer, I thought, snuggling deeper under the covers. Then I remembered what my mom had said, and I picked up the phone.

"Hi!" Gerry said, in a low voice. "I've been out with Ryan."

"So I heard. What time is it, anyway?"

"Oh, it's not the witching hour yet. I just got home and found this note to call you. Problems?"

"Mark knows, Gerry. He guessed."

"He did?" She sounded pleased.

"Maybe I'm not a very good crew. Or whatever. Anyway, he knows."

"I've still got Ryan fooled."

"No kidding!"

She caught the sour note, and said quickly, "I'll tell him soon, if he doesn't guess." She hesitated. "Any other news?"

"Oh, yes, I nearly forgot," I said, with elaborate sarcasm. "The nut called again."

"Who?" she said, after the tiniest pause.

That pause gave her away. "You know who!"

"What did he/she/it say?" She was trying to be casual about it but I could tell she was shaken. It had been only four days, but in some ways I knew Gerry like I knew myself.

I told her what the Voice said. It wasn't something I could easily forget.

There was a silence. Then she said, still in that false, light voice, "So you hung up."

"I said, 'Then do it, or I'll call the police!' And *then* I hung up."

"You said you'd call the police?" Her shock was genuine, and so was her fear. I could feel it shivering along the wires toward me when she breathed, "Oh-h-h, Gilly!"

Her panic frightened me. "Gerry, what have you done?"

"Nothing!" There was no pretense in her tone or emphasis.

"Then why is someone calling up and saying dumb things about vengeance?"

"Oh, I don't know! Listen, Gil —" She caught herself. "You shouldn't have — I mean, you shouldn't pay any attention to —" She broke off again and said, in a different tone of voice, "I've got to hang up now, Gerry, I'll call you again, okay?"

The line went dead and slowly I replaced the phone. What was my twin hiding from me?

I did not sleep well that night, and it was the telephone that wakened me again the next morning. I thought Gerry was calling back, as she had promised, but it was Mark's deep voice with a smile in it that said, "Gilly?"

"Yes — I mean *no!* Don't *do* that!"

He laughed. "Relax. I know Gerry has a private line. I have to drive down to Stanford University this morning. Want to go along for the ride? I won't be long. Just some paperwork. Did you know I am registered for the fall semester there?"

"No. That's great!" I was glad that he wasn't going off to some eastern school — for Gerry's sake, I told myself. "I'd like to go with you, Mark."

"Good. It will be warm in Palo Alto," he warned me. "In the bay area we can go from winter to summer in July just by driving out of the fog."

"Yeah, I know. It's not like the valley, where it's July for six months!"

Mark laughed.

It was thoughtful of him to warn me, I mused, putting on a pretty cotton dress I found in Gerry's closet, and picking up a sweater. My uncle had left for work but Aunt Kara was at her telephone desk when I came downstairs. She lifted her pencil in a salute and smiled at me over the mouthpiece.

"Good morning —" I had my mouth open to say "Aunt," but stopped and mumbled "Kara."

She gave me a sharp look. "Twelve-thirty, then," she said into the phone and hung up. "Morning, dear. Any plans for today?"

"I'm driving down to Stanford with Mark, just for the ride. He has paperwork down there."

"That will be pleasant. I won't be home for lunch, but you will probably lunch out, too, won't you?"

"I hope so," I said, with a grin, and she laughed. She was already tapping another number with the eraser end of the pencil, so I went to pour some coffee and fix my breakfast. She was still telephoning when Mark came to pick me up.

He was wearing a light jacket over his sport shirt and his dark hair looked as if it were still damp from his shower. His eyes went swiftly over me and my heart fluttered when I saw the approval in them.

Aunt Kara put down the phone. "Hello, Mark. What did you think of Gerry's twin?"

A look of mischief crossed Mark's face. "Wow!"

I flushed, and they both laughed. Aunt Kara went on, "Amazing, isn't it? I had girl friends who were twins when I was dating Justin. Those two led their boyfriends on a merry chase! Those boys never knew which twin they were with."

"Sounds like fun," I heard myself say. I did not dare meet Mark's eyes. Was I wrong about Aunt Kara? I studied her as she picked up her pencil and began tapping the next number, but her expression was innocent.

She was talking into the phone when we left, and she waggled her fingers at us.

We went out to Mark's neat little two-seater. The city was still gray, but by the time we were on the freeway speeding south, the sun was burning off the fog. Soon we were driving with perfect visibility along the coastal hills, down which houses tumbled toward the bay, and the sun was shining through the car windows with summer warmth.

Mark rested his hands lightly on the steering wheel, his eyes straying from the road now and then to look at me. The day would have been perfect but for my preoccupation with the phone caller and the fear Gerry was trying to hide from me.

"Something troubling you?"

I was startled. "How can you tell?"

"You've got violet shadows under your eyes this morning as if you didn't sleep well. Either you're worried about something, or you were out too late last night." He gave me a look that made me tingle as I realized he was really wondering if I had dated someone else. But how could that make any difference to him?

"It's something that happened last night," I confessed. "I was home alone and in bed when some weirdo called on the private line." I was angry again, just remembering it. "You know, Mark, it simply infuriates me that some nut can dial a number at random and disturb one's sleep —"

All at once I remembered Gerry's indignation when she told me about the stranger yanking the string she had tied to her big toe, and her recalling that incident took on a new meaning.

Mark was looking at me strangely. "But a random caller wouldn't have had access to an unlisted number."

Gerry's private number was unlisted? I opened my mouth, then clamped it shut. Now I was sure Gerry had received other calls like the one I had taken for her. She might even know the identity of the caller. She was involved in something she shouldn't have touched, I was pretty sure, but I was not going to give her away.

Mark was going on. "Of course, if he just blindly punched buttons, I suppose he could come up with any number — once in a million times."

"And if he remembered what he'd punched and got an answer, he could do it again. He's called before, Mark. I'm sure it's the same voice."

"Perhaps you should go to the police. Was he obscene?"

"Oh, no! He quotes the Bible!"

Mark raised his eyebrows. "An 'end-of-the-world' prophet?"

"Something like that," I said, uncomfortably. I would have liked to tell Mark exactly what the Voice said, and exactly how Gerry reacted when I repeated the message to her, but if Gerry had not confided in him, I could not. I owed it to her to keep her secrets, at least until I knew what they were!

"Anyway," I said, "Gerry's the one to go to the police about it."

"You could have her number changed."

"That's the answer, Mark!" I exclaimed. "That's what I'll do."

Mark's eyes shone with approval, and I caught my breath. It would be so easy to fall in love with him! I tore my eyes from his pleasant face, looking past him at the bay, now a porcelain blue under a pale blue sky.

A crazy notion had crept into my mind. Was someone blackmailing my twin? That bit about bridling my mouth . . .

Deliberately, I put the unpleasant incident out of my mind, determined to enjoy my day with Mark to the fullest. He was so different from Ryan! It was a subtle, quite intangible difference that I couldn't put into words, but I felt it keenly.

I wondered if he were in love with Gerry. He had never called *me* pork pie.

We left the bay and drove through affluent neighborhoods into a shopping area and abruptly reached the stone gates of a drive winding off through eucalyptus trees toward a cluster of distant buildings. We left the car in a parking lot and walked toward the quad, which he said was the heart of the original campus. The old buildings which formed the quadrangle were built in California-mission style, all roofed with red tiles. At one end of the square was a chapel, entirely faced with colorful glazed tiles in a mosaic of Biblical scenes.

"The Stanfords brought Italian workmen over to do the mural," Mark told me. "They built the chapel in memory of their only son who died at the age when he should have entered college."

"It's beautiful," I said, taking a long breath, and asked, enviously, "Will Gerry go to college here, too?"

"Gerry hasn't mentioned it if she has plans. Have you applied any place yet?"

"Not yet."

"Next year's soon enough, isn't it?"

I nodded, my head full of crazy dreams about Gerry and me rooming together in a dormitory, going to classes together, double-dating (or switching our dates, just for the fun of it), and comparing notes when we came back to our room. It was so entirely different from being an only child that I was not sure whether it was what I wanted or not. I didn't think I would want to switch if Mark were my date.

We stood looking up at the colorful face of the chapel, brilliant in the sun. "I'll be in the business administration building," Mark said. "You can go inside the chapel, if you want. I'll come back here when I finish, and then we'll find a place to have lunch."

I watched him cross the quad, tall and assured, the jacket that he had removed slung over one shoulder. Then I walked around the square slowly, looking at the chapel from every angle, before I pushed the heavy door open and entered. There was something about its hushed silence, its waiting pews under the heavenly ceiling and gold leaf. I stood and let its calm atmosphere wash over me, still thinking about Mark.

I knew now why I was so attracted to him, what that intangible difference was between him and Ryan. It wasn't just that Mark was ready for college and Ryan — like Gerry and me — had another year to go. No, the difference was that Mark really listened to me, and was open and responsive to everything I said. To him I was not, would never be, just Gerry's clone.

That last was very important because I thought I was falling in love with him.

CHAPTER

SEVEN

The city is never as quiet as the country. There is always some distant hum of traffic or muted siren no matter how still the hour. So it was curious that when I woke up the next morning to the usual sounds I immediately sensed the emptiness of the house and knew I was alone.

I showered leisurely and dressed in a pair of Gerry's jeans and an oversized sweater of deep rose. It was becoming, but somehow that made me feel more lonely.

Downstairs, I found a note in Aunt Kara's handwriting on her open engagement book by the telephone:

"Gerry, darling, a committee meeting this morning and luncheon with Dede. Here are the numbers where I can be reached." The note ended with a question: "See you at dinner?"

I wondered how in the world Gerry filled her summer days.

After fixing my breakfast I called the telephone company's business office about having Gerry's private number changed. Then I made my bed and, throwing myself down on it, called Gerry to tell her what I had done.

"Oh, hi, Gerry!" she said, sounding very cheerful, and went on just as if we had not talked the night before last. "Mom told me to call you back. I tried yesterday, but you were out."

"I drove down the peninsula with Mark. I've got something to tell you."

"Wait 'til I run upstairs to my extension, Gerry."

So she wanted privacy. And why had she not told my mom she'd called me? I was beginning to revise those first, dazed, emotional impressions of my twin. Were we really that much alike?

Waiting, I could see every detail of the rooms through which she ran. She must have answered the white wall phone in the kitchen. Mom was probably sitting there at the kitchen table, hearing every word Gerry said.

I followed her through the dining room with its six high-backed chairs ringing the round table, across the hall and up the carpeted stairs, past the cheval mirror before which we had stood in each other's clothes that first day, to the Princess phone on my bedside table. I could see the tiny sprigs of flowers on my bedspread, smell the damp earth from the orchards through the open window . . .

While the reel of film rolled in my head, I was turning over in my mind the things I wanted to say to my twin. There were quite a few.

She came on airily with, "Honestly, that Ryan is a neat guy! Guess what we did last night?"

"Listen," I interrupted. "I'm having your phone number changed."

I heard a tiny catch in her breath. "Well, really! It's good of you to tell me!"

"Mark suggested it. I told him about the Voice. Gerry, he's called you before, hasn't he?"

"Who, Mark?" she said, with an incredulous laugh.

"Don't be a smart-aleck! You know I'm talking about the Voice. Has he called you before?"

"That's gross, Gilly," she muttered, dropping the blithe, high-pitched tone that was obviously affected. "How do I know?"

"You couldn't forget the Voice."

"It's stupid to think I would remember every weird call I get! I told you these things happen in the city —"

"Why don't you want me to go to the police?"

"Oh, for heaven's — why ask for a hassle like that? It's nothing, I tell you!" Her voice had tightened. Again I had the impression of barely controlled panic. What I had done had increased her fear, and it worried me.

"Gerry, is the Voice someone you know? Can't you tell me what's worrying you?"

"Where did you get your imagination?" she demanded, furious now. "You keep trying to give me a problem. There are no problems! Will you just mind your own business?"

"You made it my business, too, didn't you, when you asked me to switch places? Listen, if you're in a mess, you have to tell me. I have to know what to do. Gerry, are you in danger?"

"What television programs are you watching?" she asked, coldly. "You'd better switch to the Muppets."

"All right, if that's the way you want it, but I am going to tell Uncle Justin I'm Gilly."

She lowered her voice until I could scarcely hear her. "Please don't, Gilly! Not yet. Aren't you having fun?" she pleaded. "Isn't Mark showing you a good time?"

"What has Mark to do with what I'm asking you?"

"Listen, there will be no problem at all unless you go to the police. Promise me you won't do that!"

"So there *is* a problem."

"Not if you don't go to the police or do anything foolish like that! Promise me, Gilly, please."

"I think I should know what I'm promising, Gerry. What have you done?"

"Nothing, I swear it. I'm telling you the truth."

"Then why — ?"

"Pul-eese!" It was a desperate plea. Then, as if reluctantly admitting something, she

said, "It's really better for you if you don't know, Gilly."

Would I have given in to her if it were not so important to me to see Mark again? I don't know. I do know it was against my better judgment, but I promised to give her a few more days and said I would call and give her the new number as soon as I had it.

That night Aunt Kara cooked dinner for a change. "Shall I set the table?" I asked her, and immediately knew I had made a mistake when her eyes widened. Was it that Gerry would not have offered, or that she wouldn't have needed to ask?

I didn't find out, because Aunt Kara said, immediately, "Thank you, dear. Soup spoons. Salad forks, too. I'm making your favorite."

My favorite turned out to be spinach leaves with feta cheese, which I had never tasted before, and sliced fresh mushrooms and sunflower seeds. It was good.

"I heard a disquieting rumor at lunch today," Uncle Justin said, from his end of the table where he sat with his back to the bay window. "I heard Lisa had asked for a divorce."

"Who said that?" Aunt Kara demanded.

"Albers said his wife heard —"

"Oh, those gossiping biddies! It isn't true, of course. Lisa would have told me."

Uncle Justin shrugged and began talking of something that had happened at his office. I ate in silence. It was all I could do, for I knew none of the people they mentioned and had no idea of what went on in Uncle Justin's office.

"Isn't tomorrow your ride, dear?" Aunt Kara finally asked, and I nodded.

"What ride?" Uncle Justin asked me, but Aunt Kara answered him.

"The Bike-a-thon for Pets. A sixteen-mile bike ride. You remember, *you* sponsered her and so did Herb Pound."

"So did my loyal secretary. Are you going to cost us each sixteen dollars, Gerry?"

"I'll try."

"Well, don't try too hard," he said, and then grinned at me so warmly that I was uncomfortable, remembering my refusal to forgive him for separating Gerry and me when we were young.

Mark called for me the next morning at six o'clock. I was creeping down the stairs trying not to wake Aunt Kara and Uncle Justin when their door opened quietly. Kara came to the head of the stairway in a creamy silk wrapper, her face shiny and her eyes half-open. "I'll be home this afternoon, hon. Want to call and tell me how many miles you make?"

"Sure, Kara."

She yawned. "Luck," she said, and blew me a kiss.

By the time I got Gerry's bike out of the garage, Mark was there with his bicycle on a rack on his car.

"Hi, beautiful!"

"Beautiful yourself," I retorted, smiling at him. He was wearing a jogging suit and looked squeaky clean, as if he and the suit both had just been laundered.

The warm glow in his eyes turned to faint anxiety. "Have you ridden Gerry's bike before?"

"No."

"It's geared up pretty high. Why don't you take a spin up the street before I load it?"

"I'm an experienced biker, Mark."

"Pardon me! But don't go showing off," he warned me with a glint. "Gerry's not that good."

"There's no pleasing you, is there?" I grumbled.

All the while we tossed words at each other our eyes were speaking another language, and my heart was behaving so erratically that I was having a little trouble with my breathing. Mark was pretty cool, but I could tell he was enjoying himself.

He loaded the bike, and we drove through the usual morning fog to Golden Gate Bridge Plaza where we were to meet some of the other bikers for breakfast. Sheilah was in the restaurant, looking waiflike beside a yellow-haired boy who was a head-and-a-half taller than she was. She waved at us, and we crowded into the booth with them and ordered ham and eggs.

"That's a big breakfast for a little girl," Mark teased Sheil when our heaping plates arrived.

She eyed her food with satisfaction. "You can't bike on coffee and toast."

"Sheil's Handy Proverbs, Number Twenty-Six," her date joked, and she wrinkled her nose at him. I had noticed that she did have a tendency to make grand generalizations, but in a way that was so much Sheilah that everyone, except her date, was amused.

Gerry's friends were calling to me from other booths with greetings or wisecracks. I would have been lost if Mark had not unobtrusively managed to call everyone who stopped at our booth by name. I was relieved when we left the restaurant and gathered in the parking lot with our bikes.

The man in charge rounded us up for last-minute instructions. "We're starting early in order to avoid those bridge commuters who use this parking lot," he said, "but that means we will have to deal with the phenomenon which so baffles our tourists — summer fog."

I laughed with the others, feeling like a true San Franciscan.

"However, as you know, the fog soon burns off. From here we take the road that goes down under the freeway to the Great Highway. Halfway checkpoint is at Seal Rocks Beach. Turnaround is at Fleishhacker Zoo, where box lunches will be waiting for us. Soft drinks will be available at the checkpoint."

We all cheered.

"Stay in the right lane, close to the shoulder. Several cars equipped with warning signs are accompanying us. One will precede the bikers, the others will follow. As we spread out and the faster riders are separated from the laggards, other warning cars will be inserted for your protection in traffic."

He pointed out the shepherd cars, ready in the parking lot, each with a big sign emblazoned on the rear: CAUTION! BIKERS AHEAD.

"Good luck," he finished, and we were on our way.

It was slow going at first because the road skirting Lincoln Park was narrow and hilly: a mile of climbing, then coasting a bit in order to climb again.

I was awed by the scenery. Here, just under the great bridge, its orange towers soaring out of the morning mists into an azure patch of sky were unforgettably, massively impressive. On our left the wooded park climbed to a crest, where we glimpsed the white facade of the Palace of the Legion of Honor before which, in fog or in sun, Rodin's *Thinker* forever rests his elbow on his knee and his chin in his hand.

When we finally coasted down to the broad boulevard along the beaches, we spread out as the bikers with heavier equipment forged ahead. Mark stayed by my side, pedaling easily, talking little, and keeping a watchful eye on the traffic. The sun was boring through the gray swirls, and by the time we reached our checkpoint at Seal Rocks, its warmth and our exertions had made us all thirsty.

We milled around, drinking pop — as my dad called it — and watching the sleek furred seals clamber over the rocks offshore while our names were checked against a list. We had come four miles.

"The next four will separate the boys from the men," Sheil observed, sagely.

"You mean the girls from the boys," her date said, and she hissed, "Antifeminist!"

"Oh, no, not me! I *like* the girls!"

"Yeah, in chains."

We laughed at Sheil, but she gave me a look which said she was only half-joking. Mark was not like that, I thought. He was stripping off his jogging pants, revealing his straight, strong legs, already tanned below his khaki walking shorts. He looked great whatever he was doing. My twin sister was so lucky, I thought, with a twing of jealousy. What would happen when she came back? Would I ever see Mark then?

There were fewer of us after we left Seal Rocks, and the farther we rode, the farther ahead Mark and I surged. The cool ocean air was exhilarating to one used to the summer heat of the valley, and I felt as if I could ride all day. Even Sheilah and her date were falling behind, and one of the warning cars moved up to trail us.

We had rounded the peninsula and were traveling along the ocean now, with sand dunes on our left and the Pacific rolling in to break in surf on the rocky beaches on our right.

Ahead of us loomed the zoo and the end of the Great Highway, which narrowed into two lanes before it became an on-ramp to the coast freeway. Our turnaround! We had made it halfway. Eight miles to go.

"Look out!" Mark cried, and careened across the pavement right in front of me. I had no choice except to turn my wheel onto the sandy shoulder. Even so, my front wheel tangled with Mark's rear wheel as we hit the sand.

I went over my handlebars in a somersault, the drawn-out shriek of brakes in my ears. Belatedly, I realized what had happened. A driver coming up from the rear had swung around our shepherd car and headed back into our lane.

Quickly, I rolled away from the road, praying he would not run over Gerry's bike. Mark was sprawled in the sand just beyond me.

The car had skidded a wheel off the pavement and was sitting at right angles to the lane, effectively blocking it. I sat up and found myself facing a dull maroon left-rear fender, flecked with gray primer. The shepherd car swung wildly around him. Then the driver of the maroon car, whom I could not see, gunned his motor. With a jerk the wheel I was staring at spun on the pavement. The car turned sharply left and sped back toward San Francisco.

I looked over at Mark and was relieved when I heard him calling the driver a few choice names. He was not hurt. We picked ourselves up, and I tried to brush the sand from my clothes.

We were both shaken, but as we looked at each other laughter seemed the only possible reaction. Perhaps it had happened too quickly to frighten us, but the man who came running from the shepherd car, the father of one of the bikers, was not amused. He was pale with rage.

"Did you get his license number!" he demanded, before he even asked us if we were hurt.

"Z-T-C —" I began, hesitantly.

"Or ZTO," Mark said. "He got away before I could read the numbers."

"His license plate was filthy dirty," I explained.

The man had a hand radio and he began talking into it, while Mark and I picked up our bikes and shook the sand out of the wheels, then rolled them back to the pavement. They did not seem to be damaged.

Sheil came up, pedaling furiously. "What happened? Are you okay?"

"Just a minor upset," Mark told her.

I was trying to be as cool as he was about what had happened, but I was really shaken up. I wished I had seen the driver of the car. "Was he drunk, do you suppose?" I asked.

"Either drunk or mad," Mark said, shrugging. "Where's your date, Sheil?"

She grinned wickedly. "He dropped out. No stamina."

I knew I would be sore from the rude spill,

but I resolved to say no more about it. We rode three abreast to the turning point at Fleishhacker Zoo, and all three of us were among the twenty who reached Seal Rocks for the third check.

The last four miles were the hardest, for we had to climb from the beach back up to the bridge plaza. Sheil dropped out at the Rocks, but the challenge in Mark's eyes reminded me I had bragged I was an experienced biker, so I set out again.

It was rough going. Just when it was the roughest, Mark pulled out a packet of walnuts and raisins and handed it to me. "Here's some energy, Gilly."

I don't know whether it was the packet or his encouragement that did it, but Mark and I were among the half-dozen who made the sixteen-mile trip.

"Way to go, Gerry!" a strange boy yelled as we dragged into the parking lot. I glanced at Mark and he grinned at me.

Would Gerry have made it? I wished Mark would tell me, but I didn't want to ask. I felt wonderful as I headed for the telephone booth to call Kara.

As we were getting into Mark's car, the man who had seen our accident came over to tell us that the police had been given a description of the car that had run us off the pavement, but that he didn't think they would do anything about it since we were not hurt. "Without a license number . . ." He shrugged, unhappily.

When we were driving home, Mark asked lightly, "Do you make a practice of falling down steps and off bicycles?"

I retorted, "I don't think I am especially awkward, or accident-prone, if that's what you're asking!"

"I guess I was, but don't be mad."

"I'm not mad. Just edgy, I guess."

"Any particular reason?"

Was he asking me if I had heard again from the Voice? I didn't want to think about that now. "Yes, there's a reason," I snapped. "San Francisco *does* seem to be dangerous to my health! And I'm bone-tired."

Mark sighed, and admitted, "So am I." Then he reached over and took my hand and held it all the way back to Uncle Justin's house.

CHAPTER

EIGHT

Unfortunately, I forgot to tell my aunt and uncle I had ordered Gerry's telephone number changed. The following day when the repairman arrived, late in the afternoon, they were not only home early but had brought in a few friends for a casual cocktail. We sat in the spacious living room on the second floor, with its cool earth colors and its two windows overlooking the bay.

There were no introductions. Aunt Kara naturally assumed I knew everyone. There was a married couple, middle-aged; there was a woman about thirty wearing very large blue-tinted glasses who, I soon discovered, was Uncle Justin's secretary; and there was Mr. Pound. They all teased me about costing them money because I had completed sixteen miles in the Bike-a-thon for Pets.

I was going to tell them about the man who ran us off the pavement when the door-knocker sounded. Aunt Kara went down the stairs to answer it. From the living room I heard her say, "There must be some mistake. I haven't ordered any telephone service."

I leaped up and ran down to the hall calling, "Wait, Kara! I called the telephone company," just in time to keep her from closing the front door in the face of a young man with a drooping mustache.

"Oh? Sorry," she told the repairman. "Come in." She turned to me. "I didn't know you were having trouble with your phone, Gerry."

"Oh, no trouble," I said, quickly. "I'm just having my number changed."

"Where's the phone, miss?" the repairman asked.

"I'll show you." I ran up to the third floor, and he followed more slowly.

It only took a few minutes because, he explained, the number had already been changed at the relay station. When I took him back downstairs, I was conscious of a silence as I passed the living room. I climbed to the landing again and turned to go back up to my room, but Uncle Justin called, "Come in here, Gerry. What's this about wanting a new number? Any particular reason?"

Reluctantly I returned to the living room and perched on the ottoman in front of Kara's chair. "Oh, I had a couple of funny late-night calls, and Mark suggested this was the easiest way to stop them." I had spoken as casually as I could, but I could see that they all jerked to attention. I began chewing on a fingernail.

"Funny how?" Aunt Kara demanded. "What did he say?"

I shrugged, embarrassed. "Nothing much."

"A heavy breather?" the married woman said, knowingly.

"No!" I said, my cheeks burning.

"When did this happen?" Uncle Justin asked me.

"Night before last was the last time."

"It's happened more than once?"

"Well — yes," I admitted.

"Gerry, when did you start biting your fingernails?" Aunt Kara said, suddenly. "I never saw you do that before."

I dropped my hands in my lap and sat up straight. I had always chewed at my fingers when I was nervous. Apparently Gerry didn't. Well, that was one difference between us. But not a difference that would be attractive to Mark, I reminded myself. It bothered me that I did not know how much my twin cared about him.

"Have you reported the incident to the police?" Uncle Justin's secretary was asking. "You should, you know."

"No use calling them now," Mr. Pound pointed out. "It has to be done immediately so they can trace the call."

"You can have the line monitored —" the other man began.

I had to stop that sort of talk. "It wasn't

that kind of call, at all!" I protested. "Actually, he quoted from the Bible."

"The *Bible!*" Aunt Kara exclaimed.

They all stared at me.

Uncle Justin said, "You'd better tell me exactly what was said, Gerry. As nearly as you can remember."

I remembered every word. Reluctantly, I began, " 'I will take heed to my ways, that I sin not with my tongue . . .' "

"Probably dialed your number at random," Mr. Pound said, shrugging. Then everyone began talking, wanting to tell his or her experience with missionaries and religious solicitors.

Uncle Justin dropped it then, and soon had them all talking about food. It seemed they were attending a meeting of their gourmet dinner club the following evening, and Aunt Kara was deciding aloud to make her shrimp *remoulade* to take for an hors d'oeuvre.

"Gerry, would you be a dear and go down to the wharf tomorrow and get some shrimp from your Italian friend?"

"Joe?" I asked, remembering the big man who had been confused because Gerry admitted we were sisters but told him we didn't live together. "Sure, I'll go down early."

They finished their cocktails and began getting ready to leave. "Why don't you come with us, Gerry?" Uncle Justin's secretary asked me, with a friendly smile. "We're going to try a new restaurant over on Union Street."

I begged off, and when I was alone went upstairs to call Gerry and give her her new number.

But I was thinking, Mark will have to have the number, too, and I opened the drawer of the table between the twin beds and took out Gerry's private telephone directory.

The directory was full of names of Gerry's friends. Eventually, all of them would be given her number. Could it travel through one of them to the Voice? Or was I holding the caller's name in my hand right now? It was possible, if I was right about Gerry knowing whose voice it was.

I saw Sheilah's number and an idea came to me. I called her. "Oh, hi, Gerry," she said. "What's up?"

"I've got a new number. Got your book handy?"

"Oh. Okay."

I could tell by her carefully noncommittal answer that she had an idea why my number had been changed, so I went on, "About my big problem —"

She interrupted me. "Don't tell me, Gerry. I've decided I would rather not know any more about it."

"But I was hoping you would have some good advice."

She did not take the bait. "Let's skip it, Gerry, okay? Congratulations on making the sixteen miles."

"Thanks. It was fun, wasn't it?"

"Oh, I suppose so. But my date was a disaster. Anyway, we made some money for the American Society for the Prevention of Cruelty to Animls, didn't we? I hope Kara's happy about it."

"Oh, she is!" I could imagine the way Sheil was twisting the hair on top of her pixieish head, and it made me laugh. We chatted a few minutes more, but I could think of no way to steer the conversation back to Gerry's "big problem," even though I had a hunch Sheil could tell me something about it.

Resignedly, I picked up Gerry's telephone directory again and turned to Mark's number. All at once a frightening suspicion stopped me with my hand on the phone. I was hearing Mark's carefully worded question about whether I was accident-prone in a completely different key.

Could Mark be the Voice?

It was so crazy an idea that I shied away from it. If Mark were involved, it could be nothing but a not very funny joke! And I didn't think Mark was the kind of guy who would play dangerous practical jokes.

But a panicky little voice in my head said that Mark was behind me when I was nudged just before that frightening fall down the gangplank of the *Balclutha*. Before that, he had almost swept me off his sailboat with the boom!

When had he discovered that I was not Gerry? Had he known before those near-accidents? Was it possible they were not the accidents they had seemed?

It was my heart that cried out, *No!* It was

telling me my own ignorance had endangered me on the Hobie Cat and that it was purely by accident that someone had crowded me on the *Balclutha*. I could completely absolve him of trying to run us off the road, I reminded myself, trying with irony to silence the objections in my head. I listened to my heart and tapped Mark's number.

"Hello?"

I said, breathlessly, "Mark?"

"Hi, Gerry. No, this is Borden. I'll get Mark."

Either I sounded exactly like Gerry, or he was assuming that any girl calling Mark was Gerry. Mom hadn't heard any difference in our voices. Our late-night caller must have thought he was speaking to Gerry. (I was convinced now the call had not been a random one.)

But it's strange about voices. When Mark came on, I immediately knew it was not his brother. I couldn't have said whether either of them was the Voice, for I was sure our mysterious caller was talking through a blanket or some dumb thing like that.

"Hi, this is Gilly," I said, in a rush. "I just called to give you Gerry's new unlisted number."

"I'm glad you called. I just tried to call you and got a 'that number has been disconnected' message."

I was happy he'd tried. I gave him the number and then asked, "Why were you calling, Mark?"

"Do I have to have a reason?" he teased.

"You could pretend to have one."

"This one is real. Tomorrow is my day to have the boat again. Want to go out with me?"

I hesitated. But I trusted him, didn't I? "I'd love to, Mark."

"I'll call for you early again. Seven o'clock?"

"Oh, Mark, I told Kara I'd go down to the wharf for some shrimp. Why don't you meet me down there — oh, but the shrimp will have to be refrigerated." I was still agitated by my crazy suspicions, not thinking very clearly.

"That's okay. We'll have breakfast down on the wharf, then I'll drive you up the hill with the shrimp, and we'll go on from there."

He sounded so masterful that I said, "Aye, aye, sir!" and he laughed.

No, my heart said. *Mark can't be the Voice.*

The damp summer fog curled around the buildings and blanketed the bay when I let myself out of the tall house the next morning. I filled my lungs with the moist air, which smelled of a curious mixture of the sea and roasting coffee. The streets were gray and still, and although it was morning, the night lamps still glowed mistily through the fog, casting mysterious gray shadows.

Few people were about as I hurried down the slanting streets toward the wharf. The

93

restaurants and shops of the garish tourist area were closed, some with iron grills drawn across their entrances.

Joe's vats were steaming, but the big, friendly Italian had apparently left them for a cup of coffee at the all-night diner. Two low hoots of a bass whistle sounded eerily from the bay, and I heard muffled shouts and the thud of crates. I walked through the passageway between two dark restaurants with their blank windows turned to the pier behind them, so I could watch the night fishing fleet come in.

A few boats were already tied up at mooring floats, and bearded fishermen in stocking caps were beginning to unload their gleaming, slippery catch.

The fog was heavier over the water and the incoming boats were shrouded in mist, with only the hazy lights at the tips of their masts visible until they suddenly emerged out of the grayness almost at the pier. It was like an old black-and-white movie, grayed and fuzzy, and that gave everything an aura of unreality. Even the boat whistles, hooting in short blasts as the vessels approached, sounded muffled in the heavy air.

Men leaped out of the arriving boats with lines to make them fast, shouting greetings and amiable insults at each other. The boats already tied up bumped softly against the groaning piers. I walked slowly over the planks, picking my way around coiled ropes and boxes of silver fish, enjoying the contrast of the lively work on the dock with the dead silence of the fog over the bay, out from which the boats were emerging one by one.

It was an atmosphere that seemed to me the essence of San Francisco, more real than her glittering towers and her fancy restaurants, and I loved the air of brooding mystery it had for me, a landlubber. Even the activity on the dock had a timeless quality in the fog that muffled the fishermen's shouts and laughter and made indistinct figures of both men and boats only a few scant yards away. The invisible circling gulls crying in a minor key added to the mood of the scene.

Suddenly a man came running along the pier toward the passageway to the street behind me. He just appeared, running out of the mists at the end of the pier, his footfalls thudding dully on the fog-wet planks. As he passed me he stumbled over a coil of rope and, flinging out an arm for balance, hit me a staggering blow that knocked me off the pier.

It happened so quickly and so unexpectedly that I could not even scream. I opened my mouth in a gasp of surprise as he hit me, but instinctively closed it as I sank into the oily, dark green waters of the bay beneath the pier. I plunged down — and down — and down, with no sound but a splash to mark my disappearance.

My eyes were open, and I will never forget the horror of that downward plunge into a greenish brown world. I passed the dark hulls of two fishing boats. I saw scaly barnacles encrusting the dark poles of the pier. There were mysterious ungainly shapes covered with a plushy, greenish brown moss. It was as if I had passed through a barrier into a totally alien environment from which I might never be able to return to the familiar scenes of my life.

Panicky thoughts raced through my mind. I had come alone to the wharf. There was no one to report me gone. Even Gerry's friend, Joe, did not know I was here.

Yet someone had seen me. I'd heard a shout just before the water closed over my head.

At last my frantic kicking began lifting me toward the surface. I held my breath, trying to look up through the dark water above me, terribly afraid I would come up beneath one of the boats.

I made out the dim bulk of the two hulls above me and kicked my way up between them. They were swinging gently in the water as men moved on their decks. One of them bumped me before I reached the surface, sending me sidewise, and I fought against an insane urge to draw in air when there was nothing but water to breathe. I thought my lungs would burst before I broke through the surface and drew a tortured breath.

Blinking the water out of my eyes, I treaded water. There were several men on the pier above me, one on his knees looking down. The pier seemed very far above me. I was drifting away from it, and I realized the tide was going out.

Now that I was on the surface, the hulls of the two boats sloped sharply up and away from me, their decks out of my reach. I struggled toward the pier support directly ahead of me, and the man on the pier lay face down and stretched his arms down to me. A man standing beside him threw a rope but it missed me, and I dared not stop struggling against the tide to grab at it. He began reeling it in for another try.

I was turning numb with cold. I thought I would drown there with men gathering on the dock to stare down at me, and I had no breath to cry, "Help me!" At last I came within reach of the round pier support beneath the prostrate man. I grabbed it, but it was so slippery with slimy, furry moss that my hands slid down it. Again I sank into that dank underwater world, and again I kicked desperately. I could see the rope, now hanging straight down into the water, but as I reached for it, another boat chugging in sent a wave that washed me further away from the pier.

Then a fisherman on the boat beside me tossed down a line with a noose in it. This time I caught it. I slipped it over my shoulders and clutched it with both hands while he hauled me up over the side.

"A close call, eh?" he said, cheerfully. It had all happened so quickly that the men on the pier had not moved, except for the one who had thrown himself face down to extend his arms to me, and his friend who had tossed the coiled rope.

I stood dripping water all over the fisherman's deck. He led me around the well holding his catch and down into his cabin. He was a short, robust man whose powerful muscles bulged through his wool jersey. He wrapped me in a khaki blanket and I sat on his bunk, shivering, while he poured coffee into an enameled cup and laced it with something from a brown bottle. It was the strongest coffee I had ever tasted, and it warmed me all the way down.

When I had finished the coffee and my shivering stopped, he took me up on deck and several men from the pier reached to help him put me ashore.

"Gerry! My God, it was you!" It was Uncle Justin's friend, Mr. Pound, stepping out of the little knot of fishermen on the dock. "Are you all right?"

I began shivering again, with relief as well as cold. It was reassuring to see someone I knew. "Just wet — and cold," I added, teeth chattering.

"I'll take you home." He slipped a bill into the hand of the fisherman who had rescued me. "Your blanket, sir? I'll return it."

"I think you saved my life," I told the fisherman, whose white teeth shone in his smile. I wanted to ask his name, but with a wave he jumped aboard his boat, and began tossing his catch into the crates on the dock.

Mr. Pound had his arm around me and was leading me to the passage between the two restaurants to the street. "We've got to get you warm and dry, Gerry."

When I saw Joe in his enormous white apron standing on the sidewalk behind his vats, I remembered. "Mark's coming for me," I told Mr. Pound, through violent shivers. How cold the bay had been! "And Kara wants some shrimp."

"Forget the shrimp. You need to get into dry clothes."

I didn't protest. I had never been so cold in my life. Mark would come to the house if he did not find me here.

In Mr. Pound's big car with the heater going, huddled in the blanket which reeked of fish, I began to feel warmer, but water was still dripping from my hair and running down my cheeks. "I'm making a mess of your fancy car," I told him.

"Forget it."

"I'm lucky you were on the pier this morning, Mr. Pound."

"I came down for some fresh red snapper for our dinner party tonight." He shifted gears, not looking at me.

It was still foggy, and now his windows were misting. Even so, I could see that he was driving along the embarcadero, passing several streets that climbed the hill. We passed Aquatic Park.

"You're not taking me home," I protested.

He looked at me then with flat gray eyes. "Isn't it time we had a talk, Gerry?"

I felt suddenly hollow. "What about?"

"You know what about, don't you?"

My heart sank. What had Gerry done? It must be something serious. I remembered her voice saying, "I've done nothing, honest!" and "It's better if you don't know anything," and thought, *Oh, Gerry!* My teeth began to chatter again.

We had passed Fort Mason and ahead was the marina. Mr. Pound stopped at the yacht harbor. "I've got some dry clothes on my boat, and we can talk there. Come on."

I let him help me, still wrapped up in my smelly blanket, down the white-painted pier and aboard the small cruiser Mark had pointed out to me. The *Black Tern.* Its cabin was snug and comfortable. But now that I was warmer, I was wishing I had insisted on waiting for Mark, who could have had me home in a few minutes. What was he going to think when he could not find me?

Mr. Pound opened a locker and took out somebody's warm caftan and tossed it at me. "There's a lavatory behind that door where you can clean up, Gerry. Give me that foul blanket." He took it with him and went up on deck, leaving me alone.

I went into the compact little lavatory and stripped off my wet clothes. Nothing but a hot shower could wash away the oily bay water with its aroma of fish and heaven knew what else! I washed my hair, too, and after I had slipped into the caftan, wound a towel into a turban.

When I went back into the cabin, I stared in shock at Mr. Pound. He had apparently returned to the cabin while I was in the shower, and he was going through the pockets of my wet jeans. "Hey!" I said, indignantly. "What are you doing?"

He held up my house key. "I'm going to get you some dry jeans." He was rolling my wet clothes up into the khaki blanket.

This was so unexpected that I stood a moment in confusion, wondering what on earth was happening. In that moment, Mr. Pound vanished through the cabin door — and locked it!

"Hey!" I yelled again.

"I'm locking you in for your safety, Gerry," he said, through the door. "I'll be back in a few minutes."

He knew Kara would be away, or he wouldn't have needed my house key! "If you wanted a private talk with me," I shouted, "why didn't you take me home?"

I don't know whether he heard me or not. The boat dipped and rose again as he jumped from it to the dock, and I could hear him striding away to his car.

Well, Gerry, I silently addressed my twin, *you should have told me what to expect. What do I do now?*

CHAPTER

NINE

How long would Mark wait for me before he drove up the hill to the house to see if I had slept in? He knew I was going to buy shrimp. Mark would ask Joe if I had been there. I remembered the big Italian man in his long white apron had been standing beside his steaming crab and shrimp vats when I came through the passageway with Mr. Pound. But had Joe seen me?

If he had, he probably had not recognized me, wrapped up in that damp khaki blanket with my hair streaming dirty bay water!

I looked around the cabin. Deep cushioned lounges that could double as single bunks were built-in around three walls. The other end opened into a neat galley. Curtains made of a Roman striped cotton were hung at the small portholes. I pulled them all back and discovered that none of the portholes would open. Even if I could have opened one, they were too small to crawl through.

A cruiser this size should have a ship-to-shore telephone, I thought. I prowled around the snug cabin and galley, opening doors and cupboards, looking for it. But if there was one, it was not in the cabin.

In the galley I found coffee and crackers and cans of peanuts and olives and Vienna sausages, party things like that. There were also lots of whiskey bottles. I remembered I had not had breakfast and was suddenly hungry. I filled the coffeepot and plugged it in and it began perking, so the boat was still hooked up to electricity at the dock.

With a mug of coffee and a bag of potato chips, I went back to one of the built-in sofas and munched while I waited for my dry jeans.

There was a full-length mirror on the lavatory door, and I looked at myself in the borrowed caftan. It was made of toweling in shades of blue and green and smelled faintly of perfume.

Had it belonged to Mrs. Pound? The scene I had imagined when I heard about her death flashed into my head — her husband catching her in his arms while her blood dripped down to the deck — why was I thinking of that? I tried to put my uneasiness out of my mind. The caftan looked fantastic on me. I decided to brush my hair dry.

What was Gerry doing? Were she and Ryan picnicking at the lake today? Swimming and canoeing? And where was Mark now? Was he looking for me? Or would he think I hadn't wanted to go sailing with him, after all?

Outside the portholes I could see that the fog was thinning in patches, letting some light through as the sun rose. It was enough to cause a glare from the fresh white paint on the deserted pier. I could see no activity at the other docks visible through the fog. I wondered apprehensively what Mr. Pound wanted to talk to Gerry about, and I wished again my twin had confided in me.

I heard their footsteps coming down the pier before I saw them. Mr. Pound was talking to someone with him and I thought, gladly, *Mark!* Mr. Pound had met Mark at the house, and Mark had come back with him!

But when they came close enough so I could see them through the porthole, I gasped. The man with Herb Pound was a young, bearded man in jeans and a heavy black sweater. He looked oddly familiar, and after a moment I realized that he was wearing the same heavy turtleneck and stocking cap worn by many of the young, bearded men I had seen unloading fish at the wharf. Had he been on the dock when I fell? But why would Herb Pound bring him here?

The boat tilted as they jumped aboard. A few minutes later the key turned in the lock of the cabin door, and Mr. Pound put his head in and threw some clothing at me. "Here you are, Gerry."

The door closed and his steps moved away.

I hurriedly dressed in the jeans and sweater he had brought. He had brought underclothing, too. He must have pawed through the drawers in Gerry's closet, since no one was in the house. The thought of that made me angry and a little sick.

On deck the two men were arguing in low tones. I overheard nothing of what they were saying until Herb Pound raised his voice in irritation. "I tell you, I know the family! There are only two children, a girl and a boy."

"And I tell you I saw two girls," the other man said, in a loud stubborn voice. "As alike as two sardines in a can!"

I froze. He didn't just resemble the fisherman on the wharf — I had seen him before!

"All right." Two pair of steps came down the deck and paused at the cabin door. "Okay, Gerry?"

"Come in," I said.

Herb Pound opened the door. He was wearing a yachting hat on his well-groomed hair. It gave him a different look. Until now I had thought of him merely as an unhappy widower of my uncle's generation. Now I remembered my disquieting impression of hardness the first time he looked at me, running down the stairs from Uncle Justin's study. I'd put that chilling expression down to a preoccupation with his recent tragedy. Now I reminded myself he'd thought he was seeing Gerry. Had that look in his eyes been for her?

I looked at him more closely, trying to figure out what might have happened between him and Gerry. Although he was all of forty, my dad's age, he was still handsome in a squarish, prosperous way — a strong, virile man who looked civilized and successful — and somehow dangerous.

What was the connection between him and the hairy young fisherman Gerry and I had seen the first day she took me down to Fisherman's Wharf, the one who had amused us by exclaiming, *"Two, by gawd!"*? Gerry had not given any sign she knew him.

"That's her!" The young man stood in the doorway and jerked a thumb at me. His eyes were heavy-lidded and watchful, like a snake's. "That's one of 'em. She's a twin."

I shivered. Hadn't he been in line at the *Balclutha* that day I'd gone sailing with Mark, and we'd ended up at the museum ship? Could he be the person who had nudged me just as I started to descend the ladder? And the fisherman who had run toward me out of the mist, knocking me off the pier this morning — he had been heavily bearded, too!

Herb Pound looked from him to me. It must have been obvious that I remembered the fisherman. "Who was with you that day, Gerry?"

"I'm Gillian," I said. "I'm the twin."

Herb Pound's dark gray eyes turned almost black with menace. "Don't play games with me, Gerry Partridge!"

"I'm not playing games, Mr. Pound. My

106

name is Gillian Topper. Gerry and I were separated at birth, and adopted."

He studied me, anger glinting in his gaze. "Are you saying that Justin Partridge is not your father? Come on, Gerry, do you expect me to believe that?"

"It's true, Mr. Pound. We didn't know ourselves until last week. Our parents are dead. Our mother was Justin's sister. I live with another sister and her husband."

"You say you didn't know. Why were you told now?"

"Because Gerry needed a passport for their trip to Europe, and she saw her birth certificate for the first time."

For a long moment Herb Pound said nothing, just screwed that gimlet gaze deep into me. Then he said, softly, "Damn! It fits. And that explains Justin's trip to the valley last weekend. But why the switch? What are you doing here, Gillian?"

"You tell me!" I suppose it was because Herb Pound had come to Gerry's house as a family friend that it took me so long to put two and two together. Now, something in that soft voice had made me start to tingle with dread. I exclaimed, *"You're* the weirdo who calls on Gerry's private line!"

I was sorry the minute I'd said it. Things were becoming clear too swiftly now.

"So you know about those calls," he said, his eyes narrowing. "Of course. Gerry told you who was calling."

"No," I protested. "I just now guessed. I took the last two calls."

"And threatened me with the police." His tone was icy now. "What else did she tell you?"

"She told me nothing! I guessed it was you!"

His handsome face flushed with anger. "Don't try to lie to me. Where is Gerry now?"

"I don't think I'll tell you that, Mr. Pound. I don't know what's between you and Gerry, but it has nothing to do with me." I turned away, trying to be casual. "Thanks for bringing me dry clothes. You can take me home now."

"You're not going anywhere," he snorted. "Is she in Merced?"

I tried to keep my face expressionless. Uncle Justin had made a quick business trip to Merced that Saturday they had brought Gerry to visit me.

Mr. Pound jerked his head at the young fisherman and they left the cabin. I ran after them, but before I could reach the door he had slid it shut and locked it again.

Suddenly I was very frightened. And I had thought Herb Pound was being kind when he put his arm around me and led me to his car! I should not have been so trusting but, after all, one instinctively trusts a man who looks like Herb Pound, a man who dresses well, who looks prosperous and gentlemanly — and besides, is a family friend!

The fisherman was something else. His dark eyes had been coldly impersonal, telling Mr. Pound that Gerry had a twin. I was suddenly sure it was his outflung arm that deliberately knocked me off the wharf into that numbingly cold and dirty water when the tide could have carried me under a boat. I had come so near drowning!

I was just as sure he was no fisherman. And when I was rescued, by a real fisherman, Herb Pound had been conveniently near. A cold fear enveloped me. It had occurred to me that Herb Pound had known Mark and I were going to visit the *Balclutha* that day I was pushed off the gangway ladder. Had he sent the bearded man to follow us?

Herb Pound had been at the house last night when Kara asked me to go down to the wharf for shrimp! He had been sitting there, listening, when Uncle Justin made me tell him what the Voice said, when we talked about going to the police. . . . Was that why he had brought me here?

Why did Herb Pound want Gerry dead?

The terrible question just appeared in my mind like skywriting. But once it had entered it would not go away.

And now he was here with the bearded fisherman. I could not swear it was the same man who had knocked me off the pier this morning, but all my instincts that were now clamoring I was in danger told me he was the one. The cold eyes staring at me over the brush of dark hair had revealed that he didn't care whether I lived or died. They were the eyes of a killer.

109

And the connection between Mr. Pound and the black-bearded young man who had probably posed as a fisherman was clear. Herb Pound was no longer trying to hide it. I did not want to face the awful truth I was glimpsing — it was too terrifying.

What made it worse was the conviction slowly pushing itself into my mind that my twin sister had known she was in danger when she begged me to change places with her.

Gerry, how could you?

CHAPTER

TEN

I heard them leave. Once again I was alone, locked in the cabin of the *Black Tern*. Sitting on the bunk under a porthole, I saw other boats go out from slips farther down the marina, but no one came down the pier where the *Black Tern* was berthed. It was still early and few people were about.

Two men walked down the next pier and jumped aboard a small sailboat. I took off my shoe and pounded on the glass of my porthole trying to get their attention. If only I had worn heels instead of sneakers! The men never looked my way, pushing off and moving out of my vision.

I had to get off the boat before Herb Pound and his friend returned. What could I do? How could I get a message from the boat that I needed help? Help! *SOS!*

I went to the lavatory and found a piece of soap. With it I wrote *SOS* on every porthole, carefully drawing the S backward. Then I looked around for something heavy. In the galley I found a cast-iron skillet and brought it back with me. If someone, anyone, neared the boat again, I resolved I would break the glass in a porthole. I slipped the skillet under a cushion. After that, there was nothing to do except curl up on the bunk and wait for someone to come along.

But an hour passed and the closed cabin grew warm and stale. I must have fallen asleep, for the next thing I was aware of was the movement of the boat when someone jumped from the pier onto the deck. I could hear Herb Pound—I hoped it was Mr. Pound and not his bearded friend!— moving around on deck but he did not come near the cabin. Listening to the sounds he made, I realized he was preparing to cast off.

Oh, no! Where was he planning to take me? I pounded on the door. "Hey, out there! Open this door!"

Whoever it was paid no attention to my yells. The motor roared into life, and the boat began to move out of its slip. I began screaming.

"Let me out! Put me ashore! I'm not going anyplace! Open this door!"

I dug out the skillet and pounded on the door with it, but there was no response. The pier moved steadily away until I could no longer see it through my porthole. The Golden Gate Bridge, rising out of the mist into sunlight, arched out of my sight. We were out of the marina, and the *Black Tern* was turning right. The bridge disappeared and grim Alcatraz Island came into view. We were headed toward East Bay.

Now steps approached the cabin door and the key turned in the lock. Herb Pound came in, his face grim. He had changed into some old baggy slacks and a worn sweater, making him look even less like Uncle Justin's prosperous friend. He grabbed my arm, pinching it so tightly that my grasp weakened on the skillet, and it slid to the floor. He pulled me with him into the lavatory, holding me while he filled his pockets with the small bars of soap I had found. Then he wet a sponge and thrust it into my numbed hand.

"Wash every porthole," he ordered, and pushed me so roughly I staggered back down on the bunk. My arm felt bruised where he had held me. He stood in the doorway until I had washed away every *SOS*. Then he walked out of the cabin, leaving the door open.

I rushed out on deck after him. Herb Pound was back at the wheel. Some fishing gear lay on the deck. I picked my way over the poles and tackle boxes and went forward.

A stiff breeze was beginning to dissipate the morning fog, but the foghorns were still moaning somewhere near the bay bridge. The sun was shining in patches on the houses marching up San Francisco's hills and on her splendid towers. I could hear invisible cars moving along the marina where fog hugged the shore. A factory whistle pierced the hum of traffic and the splash of our wake.

113

On our left, the grim fortress of Alcatraz and the gentle hump of Angel Island thrust up through the mists lying on the water.

It was a typical San Francisco morning with no hint in it of the desperate danger I faced aboard the *Black Tern*. But I was determined not to show my fear. "Mr. Pound," I said, "Aunt Kara and Uncle Justin will be worried. Mark will be worried. Please take me home."

He looked out toward the Berkeley hills, thoughtful and intent, ignoring me.

"I don't know what your quarrel is with Gerry, and I don't want to know. Take me home now, and I'll say nothing about what happened."

"Nothing has happened," he said absently, "yet."

He still had not looked at me, and that made the casual words seem heavy with menace. I jumped when a bell rang. It was unmistakably a telephone, very close. There was no telephone in sight. It rang again, and Mr. Pound took some keys out of his pocket and unlocked a small cabinet down below the wheel. I stared as he flipped a switch.

"*Black Tern*," he barked.

Out of a speaker came Aunt Kara's voice. "Herb, do you know where Gerry is?"

I pushed close, trying to say, "I'm here!" but Herb Pound's arm had gone around my neck and he grabbed my face, his thumb and forefinger digging savagely into my cheeks.

He had caught my tongue between my teeth, and I tasted blood. I struggled wildly, making growling noises in my throat that I knew could not be heard over his motor, and with both hands I tried to pull his hand away.

He was saying, "Isn't she at home?"

"No." Aunt Kara sounded worried. "She was to meet Mark this morning down on the wharf. Joe — you know, the crab and shrimp man? — told Mark that she had fallen off the pier and been fished out and that you drove her home."

"That's right," he said, calmly, while I struggled to break free. "She was freezing. She wanted to wait for Mark and get your shrimp, but I thought she should get into dry clothes right away."

"Her wet clothes are here." I could hear Aunt Kara's faint sigh. "She must have changed and gone out again. Did she say anything about going back to the wharf, Herb? It would be like her to go back for my shrimp."

"No, Kara, she didn't say." I heard him with disbelief. Couldn't Aunt Kara tell he was lying? "I dropped her off at the house, then took the boat out for some fishing. Can I do anything?"

He sounded really concerned. I wished I could bite him! My paralyzed jaws ached in his savage grip.

"No, thanks, Herb. She's probably with a friend. Hope you get some fish."

"Sure. I'll stop by when I come in."

Aunt Kara had been more anxious than she wanted to say. I could tell.

Mr. Pound flipped the switch, then let me go. I lunged for the switch, and he knocked me sprawling. While I was picking myself up from the deck he locked the cabinet and pocketed his keys. I eyed the cabinet hungrily. I had to get my hands on that phone!

Mark must have called Aunt Kara at the museum, which meant he knew something was wrong. Maybe Aunt Kara had sensed something was wrong, too. At any rate, she had been worried enough to leave the museum and return home. She kept so terribly busy that I had begun to think she didn't care about Gerry. I had been wrong.

The bad news, and it made my knees tremble, was that I knew now that Herb Pound had no intention of ever putting me ashore. Perhaps he had never meant to, but now that I had heard that conversation, he could not possibly let me go.

I leaned against the rail and watched the towers of San Francisco wheel around each other as we moved along the shore, waiting for the tall, narrow house above Fisherman's Wharf to appear and wondering shakily if I would ever again step through its bright door. Or ever again see Gerry — and I had just found her!

I thought about that, thought about the companionship I had missed as a child. Now I would never know it, because even if I escaped Herb Pound's plans for me, could I ever trust Gerry again?

I remembered how I had bitterly accused Mom of depriving me of that companionship the day she told me how Uncle Justin had insisted on taking Gerry. "You could have let me go with her."

"Oh, honey!" Mom said, and I knew I had hurt her. Would I ever see her and Dad again?

Should I go over the side and try to swim for shore? I remembered my descent into the numbing dark water this morning and shuddered. Wouldn't I be giving Herb Pound the opportunity he wanted to create an "accident"? The current was swift here between Alcatraz and the shore. I had heard that very few prisoners who tried to leave Alcatraz by swimming to shore escaped with their lives.

I heard the distant ring of the mobile phone again, but I did not move from the rail. Instead I watched closely, noting which pocket held Herb Pound's keys, which key he used, and which switch he flipped on. He made no attempt to keep me from interrupting this conversation, and that was frightening, too.

In a moment I knew why and was even more scared. A man said, "Nothing in Merced," and I guessed the voice was that of the dark-bearded fisherman.

"Damn!" Herb Pound said. "I was sure Partridge mentioned a visit to a sister in Merced. I don't think it was Modesto, but I know it starts with *M*."

He was trying to find Gerry! I trembled

with a cold fear. What were they planning for her?

"Madera? Manteca? There's a whole string of towns along Highway 99 starting with *M!*"

"Hell, they're all the same to me," Herb Pound said. He looked at me. "Is it Madera, Miss Gillian?"

I opened my mouth and screamed.

Over our heads the gulls screamed back at me. The small craft between us and Alcatraz moved around the island with no sign anyone aboard had heard me. Herb Pound gave me a mocking smile.

"Try Madera, then," he said into his phone.

He switched it off and locked the cabinet again. Then he pulled out a pipe, tamped tobacco into it, and lit it with his back to the wind and his hands cupped over the bowl. The *Black Tern* chugged leisurely along, paralleling the shore.

The wind was too brisk for small sailboats and patches of fog still hung over the bay. Somewhere beyond Telegraph Hill the lone foghorn was sounding periodically. Under the bay bridge appeared a large gray ship with a strange flat silhouette and some curious objects on its deck. It was coming toward us, growing larger and larger — an aircraft carrier!

I could see the white hats of sailors, some moving on deck among the tied-down planes. It sounded a short hoot of its deep horn, and Herb Pound answered with a short blast of his whistle. It was going to pass right by us on its way to the Golden Gate. Port to port, I thought. Mark had taught me that much.

I stood at the rail, staring up. The great ship loomed above us, stories high. The white-capped sailors on the deck were looking down at us. I began waving wildly, and a sailor pointed at me. But he was smiling. I cupped my hands to my mouth and shouted, "Help! I'm a prisoner!"

Herb Pound tilted his head, grinning up at them, and waved his pipe. A cheer went up, and then the sound of male voices, singing. Faintly, the strains of "Aloha Oe" wafted down to us. I caught my breath on a sob. They thought I was waving a farewell to them! Herb Pound laughed as the big vessel cleared his cruiser and steamed toward the Gate and Honolulu.

The fog was almost burned off now. Over against the east shoreline a few large sails were appearing. As soon as he was clear of the carrier's wake, Herb Pound turned north around Angel, putting the island between us and the San Francisco shore. There, in what Mark had called the Tiburon Channel, he cast out the anchor and dropped in a fishing line. But he kept near the wheel and the mobile phone cabinet. I stayed on deck, tensely waiting for another boat to come within hailing distance and frantically trying to figure out some way to get Mr. Pound's keys.

An hour passed, and the telephone signaled again. The fisherman's voice came over the speaker. "Nothing in Madera. I'm going up to Modesto."

I had crept close, hoping to cut off the connection. Mr. Pound grabbed my arm in that fierce, bruising grasp again. "You'd better talk, young lady! Is it Modesto?"

"Y-yes," I stuttered.

He studied my face and said into the phone, "Skip Modesto. Get on to Manteca. And don't be all day about it!"

I froze, and Herb Pound laughed. "Your eyes give you away, Miss Gillian." He flung me aside and locked up the telephone.

A few small sailboats had put out from Tiburon and Sausalito, but none came within hailing distance. A large white ferryboat moved out from its San Francisco pier and came slowly across the bay toward Sausalito. I could see men and women strolling the decks and standing at the rail, so near and yet beyond my reach.

Another hour passed. I jumped when I heard the signal of the mobile telephone.

It was the same voice, answering to Herb Pound's, *"Black Tern!"*

"There's a Topper family in Manteca, and the city directory says there's a daughter named Gillian. I'm on my way to the address now."

"Don't even drive by it!" Mr. Pound said sharply and warned, "I don't want any slip-up!"

"I know you don't, and don't forget I know why." There was a soft but unmistakable threat in the voice.

Mr. Pound swore into the phone.

"Trust me," the man said, while I stood transfixed with horror. "I know my business."

He would be waiting for Gerry when she came home. Or he would be following her when she left the house. And he knew his business. I was afraid to think about what his business was.

Perhaps, I thought desperately, I could warn her through that strange communion of our minds. It was true that twins had a special closeness. More than once in this last fantastic week I had had the curious feeling that I had entered Gerry's mind. If ever I could do it again, now was the time.

I concentrated. *Gerry, a man is looking for you. I think he is a killer. Please, Gerry, tell my mom what this is all about. Ask her to call the police and tell them —* what?

Tell them to come and get me off the Black Tern!

CHAPTER

ELEVEN

Herb Pound locked up the mobile telephone and hauled in his anchor. He started the motor and the *Black Tern* began moving around Angel Island. The fog had burned off over the bay and the hills of Marin County, but a great rolling bank of gray lay outside the Gate. We were headed toward it.

I knew I would not come back.

Never see Mark again. Or Gerry, my other self, who was even now being stalked by a killer. Or the two people who had been real parents to me — Mom and Dad, whom I knew I could never think of as Aunt Judy and Uncle Garth.

Ahead of us on our right was Belvedere, with its mansions hidden in layers of foliage, hiding Sausalito from our view. And beyond it was the Marin anchor of the Golden Gate Bridge, coming closer and closer.

What was it that Gerry knew? Something so dangerous that it was costing both our lives. I drew in my breath sharply as I realized what it must be. It had been no accidental shot at a gull that had hit Herb Pound's wife that tragic day on this very deck. It had been a sharpshooter's deadly aim, and Herb Pound must have known it was coming.

And that same sharpshooter was waiting for Gerry now!

I clutched the rail and clenched my teeth to keep from crying out hysterically what I knew. All at once I realized how vulnerable I was there at the rail and I was frightened, terribly frightened. A few swift steps, and Herb Pound could dump me over into those swirling gray waters and in seconds be back at his wheel.

Yet I would be no safer in the cabin for there he could do whatever he wished, out of anyone's sight. Out here at least we were visible, perhaps, to some bird-watcher in one of those mansions, or to some sailor under one of those sails with a pair of binoculars. Herb Pound could not be sure. I realized he would not do anything violent until we had passed through the Golden Gate and were safely hidden behind that curtain of fog. But we were steadily nearing the Gate.

I stayed at the rail, trembling, praying one of the many sails now visible near the shore would come closer. And then I saw it, a small red dot that seemed to be growing. I watched incredulously as it grew larger and larger. It was a catamaran, skimming across the bay much faster than the *Black Tern*, which was chugging along with the air of a pleasure cruiser with all the time in the world. The Hobie Cat was tacking back and forth but rapidly closing the gap between us.

I tore my eyes away from its red sail, fearing my riveted attention would warn Mr. Pound. But out of a slanting glance I saw the black logo: *DO4*.

Dolan Four. It was Mark!

My heart sang as the catamaran skimmed silently over the water like a butterfly darting over a pond, steadily gaining on us. As little as I knew about it, I could see that Mark was a superb sailor. Mr. Pound must have seen the red sail now, but he did not increase our speed. He just kept the *Black Tern* on course for the Golden Gate. We were near enough now to see the cars moving smoothly and swiftly across the bridge far above us.

The water had grown rougher as we came nearer the Gate. The catamaran was tilting up and down on the short choppy waves like a rocker. Anxiety tightened my chest until I could hardly breathe as Mark made a daring pass so close to us I could see the taut muscles of his jaw. He had on a pair of tight jeans and a windbreaker with a hood that lay back on his broad shoulders. His dark hair was tossing in the wind and his face was grim with concentration.

"Stand off!" Herb Pound shouted, and blew a warning blast of his whistle.

"Come aft, Gilly!" Mark yelled.

I ran to the stern and waited while he tacked away and then skimmed up behind the cruiser. He stood on the canvas with his legs wide apart and threw a bowline to the cruiser not far from where I stood. I ran to slip the eye of the bowline over the cleat on the deck, looping the end of the line around and around before securing it with a hitch the way I had seen Mark tie up the Hobie Cat that day we sailed to Sausalito.

Pulling on the line, Mark was snugging the *Dolan Four* up against the cruiser. When he had secured the cat to the cruiser, he reached up and hoisted himself aboard.

"Oh, Mark!" In relief, I threw myself at him, and he hugged me tightly. I closed my eyes, savoring the comfort of his strong arms holding me close.

"So you found us," Herb Pound said behind me, and Mark let me go.

"Yes, sir. Where are you headed? It's pretty foggy outside the Gate, isn't it?"

"We're not going far." He was walking toward us.

I saw the knife in his hand, and screamed, "Mark!"

Mark pushed me behind him and crouched, facing Herb Pound.

Mr. Pound laughed. Casually, he walked up and sliced the line, setting the *Dolan Four* adrift. "Glad you joined us, Mark," he said.

My eyes met Mark's in terror. I knew what that meant. I was not sure Mark did, although his expression had frozen in shock.

Herb Pound told him. "You've solved a problem for me. Now when you and Gillian disappear and the wreckage of your Hobie Cat washes in, Justin and Kara will think you found her and took her sailing. The Coast Guard will assume you sailed too near the Gate and were swept out to sea and washed overboard in the fog.

"In fact," he said, thoughtfully, "I think I will report how recklessly you sailed up to hail me as I neared the Gate. It's more than possible someone else was watching your show-off tacking just now."

The mobile telephone rang.

"Into the cabin, both of you," Mr. Pound ordered.

I looked at Mark. He nodded slightly. I had to walk past Mr. Pound to reach the hatch. He stepped against the wall of the cabin, making me pass him closely against the rail, and I hesitated. He still had the knife in his hand.

The phone rang again, and Herb Pound ordered me, "Move it!"

I had just reached the door of the cabin when I heard the crashing thud. I whirled around. Mark and Herb Pound were both down, grappling and rolling, as each tried to get on top of the other on the narrow deck. Mark had both hands around the wrist of the hand that held the knife. Instead of following me into the cabin, Mark had jumped Herb Pound.

The phone rang insistently through their grunts and groans and Mr. Pound's cursing.

We were headed under the Gate, and with no one at the wheel the *Black Tern* was wallowing in the choppy waves. Mr. Pound's knife clattered to the deck. The area in which they fought was so cramped, so confining, that they had scarcely room to swing a blow. It was a silent, deadly wrestling match, which I watched for the first few seconds in helpless terror.

Then, recovering from my shock, I ducked into the cabin and grabbed the skillet up off the floor where I had dropped it.

When I came out on deck, Mr. Pound was on top of Mark and was banging his head on the deck. Mark had his hands around the older man's throat. Mr. Pound's face was flushed, but beneath him, Mark looked pale. I kicked Mr. Pound's knife out of my way, and it slid under the seat and dropped into the bilge. Then I raised my skillet and brought it down as hard as I could on Mr. Pound's head.

He collapsed on Mark, and Mark lay there for a moment breathing hard.

"Mark, are you hurt?" I cried.

"Just winded."

"Roll him over against the cabin wall."

"Bulkhead," Mark corrected me, automatically, and I giggled, hysterically.

"Steady, Gilly. We're all right now. But we must tie him up."

I was trembling, but the moment of hysteria had passed. I went forward and brought Mark the fish line. He turned Mr. Pound over and tied his hands behind him, then tied his ankles together. Then he rolled him over on his back.

"Where's that blasted telephone?" The monotonous ringing had continued all through the fight.

"Under the wheel," I told him. "The key's in his right trouser pocket."

Mark dug out Mr. Pound's keys, but by the time he had unlocked the cabinet, the phone was silent.

"That was him," I said, feeling cold. "That was the man Herb Pound sent to kill Gerry."

"What!" Mark paled. We had passed through the Gate during the fight, carried by the current. The Golden Gate was a funnel for the bay, and the tide sucked the water out with a frightening strength and speed. It had carried us into the fog bank. Foghorns were sounding from each jaw of the Gate. The sun was invisible and the cities around the bay behind us had disappeared.

"He's been trying to find her, and the last time he called he said he had the address and —" My voice broke.

"Call Gerry," Mark said, picking up an instrument that lay cradled over the speaker and handing it to me. "I have to bring this tub around before we get lost in this soup and get her back through the Gate without running into a rock, and I've never handled a boat like her before. Go on!" he said, impatiently. "Call Gerry, and then we'll call the Coast Guard."

I dialed the familiar number, seeing in my mind's eye the ranch house set down in the orchards with its neighbors scattered around it, safe and ordinary, with children playing on the lawns, their beloved dogs scampering after them — and the nondescript car with the dark stranger behind the wheel parked down the road, waiting . . .

"Mom?" I cried, when she answered. "This is Gilly, not Gerry. Gerry's with you."

"I know, dear."

"You know? You've known all along?"

"Of course, Gilly. Did you think I wouldn't?"

I strangled a sob of relief. Until then I had not known how badly I had wanted her to know me.

"What's the matter? You sound upset."

"Mom, is Gerry there with you? I mean, in the house?"

"No, dear. She's with Ryan and some other young people in Micke Park."

"Oh, no!" I wailed. "Don't let her come home! I mean, tell Pop to go and get her and take her to the police station. There's a killer stalking her."

"A —" Mom gasped. "I'm not sure I heard you, dear."

"You heard right, Mom. He's a murderer. I think he's in a car parked near the house, waiting —"

"What kind of car?" Mark asked anxiously beside me, and I turned to him.

"I don't know. But he will be parked a little way from the house. I heard them talk on this thing, and he said he knew his business."

"He did, huh?" Mark's jaw knotted, making him look much older.

I had a flash of intuition. "Mom!" I cried. "Tell them to look for a dull maroon car with a license that begins *ZTO* or *ZTC!* Tell them there are gray flecks of primer showing on the left rear fender."

"Wait a minute!" Mark said. "You don't think — ?"

"It could have been him, Mark."

Mom had heard Mark talking. She said, sharply, "Gilly, where are you now, exactly?"

"I'm under the Golden Gate Bridge, I think. It's pretty foggy —"

"Where?" she shrieked.

"Mom, I'm all right. Mark rescued me. We've got the man who abducted me tied up on the deck of his cruiser —"

"Gilly," she said — her voice had gone faint — "let me get your father —"

"Mom, don't put down the phone!"

Mark snatched it from me. "Mrs. Topper, Gilly is safe. It's Gerry we're worried about. Just do as Gilly said. Get Gerry fast and take her to the police station. She'll be safe there, and she can tell the police what it's all about."

He hung up, and looked at me. "We'd better compare notes before we call the Coast Guard. It's about the murder of Herb's wife, isn't it?"

"Mark! Did you know it was murder?"

"I've never been satisfied with the police

theory that it was a random shot. Then this morning — well, for one thing Herb's story stank. Gilly, I knew you wouldn't just run out on me without leaving any kind of a message."

His golden brown eyes flashed warmly, and I shook my head fervently in agreement. He looked ahead again, tense and watchful at the wheel, as he spoke.

"When Joe told me Herb had taken you home dripping wet, I drove up the hill to the house. I actually saw his car driving away, so when you didn't come to the door, I sat in my car and waited. That's why I couldn't understand how you could have changed clothes and gone right out again, without my seeing you."

"He brought me here, then took my wet clothes home and brought me dry ones." I blushed as Mark's eyebrows shot up, and I added hastily, "He gave me a caftan."

"He'd better not have laid a hand on you!"

"He didn't, Mark. But he wouldn't believe I wasn't Gerry at first, and then he wanted to know what she told me. I think the man who is after Gerry killed Herb's wife, and that Herb knows it. Oh, Mark, do you think he —"

"Hired the killer?" Mark asked, quietly.

"It's too horrible to think about, but when Herb said, 'I don't want any slip-up,' the man said he knew why."

"Gerry must know something that incriminates him."

"Please call the Coast Guard, Mark!"

"In a minute. I'm fighting this boat," he confessed. "It's new to me, and the current is fierce here."

But he had turned the boat around and the fog was thinning. We could see the burnt orange piers of the bridge, faint in the fog but very near. The *Black Tern*'s powerful motor was moving us steadily back into the bay. Herb Pound was still lying unconscious on the deck. I wondered how long he would be out.

I looked back at the fog bank lying beyond the Gate, and glimpsed the red sail of the *DO4* in the fog that lay against the Marin hills. It was lying low over the water and I knew with a pang that the catamaran would be smashed on the rocks there.

CHAPTER

TWELVE

Where was Gerry now? I pictured her in Micke Park with Ryan and the gang. I had been there on many picnics, and I knew the routine. First, there would be a haphazard sort of softball game, with a couple of the fellows choosing up sides, taking both guys and girls on their teams. After some riotous playing they would fall like locusts on the food, stuffing themselves on deviled eggs, fried chicken, potato salad, pickles, olives, homemade cakes, and soft drinks carried in a plastic cooler full of chipped ice. Then, stuffed with food, they would spread blankets in the sun or shade, and separate into couples for an hour of intimate murmuring, teasing, sunning, or napping.

There were always a couple of fellows like Terry Chandler and Legs Darnell who didn't bring dates and who spent their time acting the clown, jumping over the reclining couples, tickling awake the sleepers, making crude jokes. Then, when the languor of over-eating had worn off, there would be a half-hearted try at another game, ending when the sun sank low enough to shine directly into their eyes.

I thought of Gerry and Ryan driving to-ward home with the slanting afternoon light throwing long shadows from the sycamore trees that lined the road across Ryan's beat-up car, both of them tired and sweaty and totally unaware of the cold-eyed man who was waiting for them — and I couldn't bear it.

Mark was calmly talking into the tele-phone, telling the Coast Guard that we were aboard the *Black Tern* with the owner trussed up like a dangerous animal, and why. With difficulty I kept myself from screaming into the instrument while he told them about Herb Pound cutting the *DO4* adrift. Apparently, the man in the Coast Guard station asked if anyone was aboard her.

"No, sir," Mark said, and I could hear the lump in his throat. "I brought her out alone." He probably thought they wouldn't go after his catamaran because there was no one on it, and I could understand how he felt.

But it was just a boat, after all, and Gerry was my twin. I wanted to scream, *Gerry! Tell them about Gerry!*

It was only seconds, even if it did seem hours to me, before he was asking them to call the Manteca police and tell them about the threat to Gerry. I snatched the phone from him, crying, "Please, you must hurry, my sister is in terrible danger —"

"Take it easy, miss," the deep voice said. "I need some information before we can do anything."

I slowed down but answered his questions with impatience, repeating the conversation I had overheard between Herb Pound and his rough friend, as well as telling him about the Voice on Gerry's private line.

"We'll ask the police to check it out, miss," he said, at last.

Couldn't he see? "But we think he is a murderer! She could be in terrible danger!"

"Don't worry. We'll ask Manteca to send an officer out to your house."

"But she's on a picnic!" I cried, in despair. I just didn't seem to be getting through to him. "She'll be coming home soon, and she doesn't suspect —"

The man had hung up.

"Take it easy, Gilly," Mark said. "We've set things in motion. Now let's nudge them on a bit." He took the phone from me and dialed another number. "Mr. Partridge, please."

This time I flipped the switch I had seen Mr. Pound use, so I could hear the conversation. Uncle Justin's secretary was saying, "Mr. Partridge is in conference —"

"This is Mark Dolan. It's about Gerry. Interrupt him, please, no matter what he is doing."

I heard Uncle Justin's secretary gasp and

in seconds Uncle Justin said, "Mark? What's happened?"

Mark began his story again, but his voice was drowned by the hoot of a freighter coming toward us. Mark handed me the telephone, while he looked for the whistle to answer the signal.

"Uncle Justin?" I said. "This is Gilly. Gerry is in Manteca, and —"

He groaned. "So Kara was right. She suspected you two were playing games with us."

Aunt Kara suspected? Are Gerry and I not as identical as we thought? No, it isn't possible. We are a whole seed that had split into equal, identical halves. No matter how I feel about her part in what has happened to me, I feel the danger she is in as keenly as I am feeling my own.

"Kara's been terribly worried. Where are you, Gilly?"

"We're on the *Black Tern,* and —"

"Herb Pound's boat?"

"Yes. We've tied him up."

"Tied *Herb* up?" His voice had risen.

"Uncle Justin, please don't interrupt. There's a man after Gerry, because she knows something. He's the man we think Mr. Pound hired to kill his wife, and —"

Mark found the whistle and blasted it in our ears. When the sound died away Uncle Justin said, in a stunned voice, "Did I hear you say Herb Pound hired someone — I don't believe it! What the hell is this, anyway?"

"Mr. Pound kidnapped me this morning. He thought I was Gerry and when I told him we were twins he sent this man to find Gerry. He was taking me out on the ocean when Mark caught up with us and he — we knocked him out."

"Good God! Are you all right? Does Gerry know about this man who's — who's trying to find her?"

"Mom knows. Gerry's on a picnic. But the Coast Guard said they would send the police."

Mark was gesturing for me to hand him the phone. He told Uncle Justin what I had left out.

"I'll call Detective O'Brien," Uncle Justin said. "Are you headed for the marina?"

"Right. But I see a Coast Guard cutter coming toward us now. I'll bring Gilly up to the house as soon as we're squared away with them."

"I'll probably see you at the police station. I'll bring O'Brien if I can get hold of him. Is Gilly really all right?"

"She's okay, Mr. Partridge."

"Who is Detective O'Brien?" I asked Mark when he had secured the phone.

"The detective who investigated Mrs. Pound's death. He questioned the Partridges because Kara and Mrs. Pound were good friends."

I stood very close to Mark as we plowed through the water against the tide in the general direction of the marina. Not a trace of fog remained in the folds of the shining San Francisco hills or on the waters of the bay. It was a beautiful day. But it was undoubtedly a typical hot summer day in the valley, too — a perfect day for a picnic — and yet a killer waited on a pleasant country road for an unsuspecting young girl and her date.

Such a cold chill came over me that I pressed even closer to Mark. "Oh, Mark, if you hadn't come! I'm safe now, but Gerry —"

Mark was looking straight ahead toward the cutter slicing the water toward us. "Did Gerry tell you she was in danger when you decided to change places?"

"N-no." I didn't want to talk about it. This was between Gerry and me.

"She must have known."

I looked up at his face. It was concentrated, and tense. "I — don't know, Mark."

An errant memory came to my mind. It was the first night I was in the narrow bayside house. Gerry and I were starting down from her third-floor room, and we could hear voices from Uncle Justin's second-floor study. "Go on down," Gerry said. "I forgot something." And she had not come downstairs until after Herb Pound had left the house.

I put the memory uncomfortably away.

Mark was saying, in a peculiar tone, "What about your boyfriend?"

I must have looked blank for he repeated, with an impatience I had not seen in him before, "Your boyfriend back home. Gerry's with him, isn't she?"

"Yes. But —" I wanted to say that Ryan was no longer my boyfriend, although he didn't know it yet. But was Mark thinking I was worried about Ryan — or was he afraid that Gerry was falling for Ryan? The warmth I had seen in his eyes could be friendship for Gerry's twin, couldn't it?

Mark didn't wait for me to finish. "I guess you're pretty worried about him, too."

"Well, yes, of course." I felt a curious relief. "But I'm afraid I've mostly been thinking of Gerry."

"Then you can't be in love with him."

There was a queer flutter in my chest. "No," I quickly agreed. I knew I was not in love with Ryan.

"I can't forget that Gerry placed you in danger," Mark said, bitterly, "without any warning."

"Mark, please don't say that," I protested, even though his concern warmed me. I understood Gerry so well. Perhaps I even understood myself better because of her. In a sense, she *was* my self. I might blame her for using me to escape San Francisco and Herb Pound, but I could not let anyone else blame her! Especially Mark.

"She's in great danger, Mark. She must know something Herb Pound doesn't want known. I can't judge her until I know what it is, and how she learned about it."

"I know. I'm terribly worried about Gerry, and I am sorry she didn't trust me enough to tell me what was frightening her." Mark ran his fingers through his blowing hair. "But the way I feel about you is different, Gilly. When I realized Pound must have abducted you — well, if anything had happened to *you* —" He looked down at me, his eyes brilliant and steady. "You're special, you know. You have been ever since that first night when I thought I was kissing Gerry and instead found a gentle, frightened girl who was a complete stranger to me in my arms."

"But we're just alike," I protested, my pleasure mingled with uneasiness. I had known I was falling in love with Mark. But was Gerry in love with him, too? *Maybe we'll find out,* she'd said. The thought that I was contemplating was unbearable when I felt like I was in her skin, riding beside Ryan to her death.

Mark was shaking his head. "You look just alike. But the essence of you is you, just as the essence of Gerry is nobody but Gerry."

"I don't think I understand that, Mark."

"I don't either, honey," he said, and the endearment sent a guilty flush of joy through me. "It is just something I feel. Physically, you and Gerry are identical, but you are still unique. I think I may be falling in love with you, Gilly. Do you mind?"

I was trembling again. This was what I'd secretly dreamed about, but it was more than I wanted to face just now. I shook my head and stepped away from him.

"I don't know, Mark. I've been through too much today. I've got to find Gerry safe and well before I'll know just how I feel."

"My feelings won't change," Mark said. His eyes, very serious, looked old in his tense young face. "Will you remember tomorrow what I said, Gilly? Whatever happens?"

There was a bellow from Herb Pound who had wakened and was pounding his bound feet against the deck. He had seen the Coast Guard cutter, passing on our port side. A sailor in its bow shouted, "Where's the catamaran?"

Mark pointed toward the Gate. "Drifting toward Marin."

"Anybody aboard her?"

"No."

"Who's the owner?"

"My father."

"We'll take her in tow."

Some of the strain left Mark's face as he nodded an acknowledgment. Behind the cutter was a smaller boat with SFPD painted on its bow. It came up swiftly and swung around us to starboard. A policeman was bawling at Mark through a megaphone to cut his throttle. Another officer was snapping pictures of Mark and me at the wheel and of Herb Pound lying trussed up on his own deck.

"Help!" Herb Pound shouted. "I've been highjacked!"

Mark shut down the engine and the harbor patrol boat moved slowly closer until it nudged the *Black Tern*. Two police officers boarded us. One of them cut the fish line binding Mr. Pound's ankles. Paying no attention to his accusations that we had highjacked his boat and tied him up, they helped him climb over the side and down to the deck of the police patrol boat. One officer followed him. The other came back to where Mark and I stood at the wheel. He was the older of the two officers and he looked like somebody's father, but with eyes so keen you knew he would never be deceived because they would miss nothing.

"I'm Officer Brundel. Your names?"

"I'm Mark Dolan. This is Gillian Topper."

He pulled a small notebook from his chest pocket and wrote in it. "All right, Mark. Take her in to the police dock. Just follow the patrol boat." Officer Brundel turned to me, his voice gentle but demanding the truth. "Are you all right, Gillian?"

I gulped. "Yes, sir." I *am all right, but what about Gerry?*

CHAPTER

THIRTEEN

Detective O'Brien was waiting at the police station when we arrived, a blond giant with a squarish face and sharp blue eyes that went immediately to mine.

"Miss Partridge," he acknowledged. "It would have been much better if you had confided in me when we first met, wouldn't it?"

"I'm Gillian Topper."

His blue eyes widened just a trifle.

"Uncle Justin didn't tell you? I'm Gerry's twin sister."

"Twins!" he said, with an expressive shrug of his big shoulders, and shook his head in a baffled way. "Mr. Partridge told me, yet you still fooled me! Then it's your sister who is in Manteca?"

"That's right." I wondered if he really had been fooled, or just wanted to know what I would say.

The door was pushed open and Uncle Justin strode in, looking worried, yet crackling with nervous energy. You just knew he would handle everything.

"Well, Gilly," he said, embracing me, "you and Gerry got right into the spirit of things, didn't you? Pulling a switch on us almost as soon as we introduced you!" He shook hands with Mark. "We are indebted to you, Mark. I've talked with the Coast Guard. They've picked up your catamaran."

Mark let out a relieved breath. "I'd hate to tell my family I wrecked it. Dad would take it okay, but my brothers would run me out of town."

"I doubt it," Uncle Justin said, smiling. "I suspect they're going to be pretty proud of you." He turned to Detective O'Brien then, the worry settling back on his face. "Any word from Manteca?"

"Not yet."

"Where's Aunt Kara?" I asked.

"She's staying close to the phone in case Judy calls. Are you holding Pound?" he asked the detective.

"He is being interrogated now. You're next, young lady." He touched my shoulder reassuringly. "Just tell the officer everything that happened."

"Everything?" I said tiredly. "That's a large order."

The big detective did not smile. "Everything," he repeated.

Mark's father had arrived by the time I was through making my statement. He looked a lot like Mark would look with quite a few more pounds and some gray hair. "So this is the twin I've been hearing about?" he said, pleasantly enough, but his eyes were so searching that I wondered what Mark had told him about me.

"Mark saved my life, Mr. Dolan."

"I'm glad," Mr. Dolan said, with something like Mark's wonderful smile.

I was drooping with fatigue. It had been an effort to go through it all again for the police. I had been so terrified, so tense all day that now I was letting down I was collapsing like a leaky balloon, even though my anxiety for Gerry was growing stronger as each hour passed without news.

Mr. Dolan said he would wait for Mark, so Uncle Justin and I left and drove back to the bayside house.

Aunt Kara met us in the foyer.

"Heard from Gerry?" Uncle Justin said, dropping a kiss on her pale cheek.

She shook her head, then put her arms around me and held me tight. "Gilly, dear! You're to call your mother at once." Her eyes were brilliant with tears.

As I walked down the hall toward the telephone desk just inside the kitchen door, the bell rang. I sprinted and picked up the phone, with Aunt Kara right behind me. "Hello?"

"Gilly, is that really you?" It was Mom and her voice was shaky. "Are you all right, dear?"

"I'm fine, Mom."

"I'm so relieved! Tell Kara the police

picked up a man in a car down the road from our place. He had pulled off under those big live oaks and was waiting —"

I drew a deep breath. "Then Gerry — ?"

My dad came on the extension. "Hello, girl, you okay?" His voice was trembling with emotion. I knew in that second how much I meant to them and how very much I loved them both.

"Yes, I'm fine. What did they do to the man?"

"They're holding him for the San Francisco police. We'll be there tomorrow to bring you home, honey. Sure you're all right?"

"Of course, I'm sure."

"Oh!" It was a glad cry from Mom. "Gerry just walked in the door, Gilly. Tell Kara, will you?"

I turned my head and cried, "Gerry's home!"

Aunt Kara lifted joy-filled eyes to Uncle Justin. But my feelings about my twin were suddenly ambivalent. Now that I knew she was safe, I stopped excusing her for the way she had used me and began to feel very angry.

"Put her on, will you, Mom?"

"Hi, how are you, Gerry?" my twin said blithely, and that did it. I was furious.

"I'm alive," I snapped, "no thanks to you!"

Aunt Kara reached a manicured hand over my shoulder, but Uncle Justin caught and held it before she could grab the phone from me.

"Hey, what's up?" my twin said. Gerry hadn't even known we were in danger! She had turned away from the phone, and I heard her say wonderingly, "Did you call me 'Gerry'?"

I grinned in spite of myself. She still thought she had Mom fooled.

"Your mother will tell you what's up," I said, deliberately, and handed the telephone to Aunt Kara. She immediately launched into a dramatic description of how worried she and Uncle Justin had been.

I listened for a moment and then realized I had had nothing to eat all day, just coffee and coffee and more coffee — a cup before I started down to the wharf to meet Mark, a mug with some potato chips on the *Black Tern*, and the plastic cup the sergeant had filled for me at the police station. No wonder my stomach burned!

But I felt too exhausted to rummage in the refrigerator, and announced to anyone who was listening that I was going to bed. Uncle Justin was sprinting up the stairs ahead of me to pick up the extension in his study. I continued up to the third floor and my twin's cool bedroom.

When I was out of my jeans and sweater I collapsed under the covers, but I was not even near going to sleep. The sun lay on the horizon and orange reflections blazed from west-facing windows all around the bay, some that I had never seen before showing up like a cat's eyes reflecting the headlights of a car.

I watched the sky's changing colors as the sun sank, thinking that this was my last night in the uncluttered bedroom with the fantastic view and the unlisted private line. Tomorrow I would go back to the house in the orchard and to a Ryan who had been perfectly happy with my twin. What would my relationship with Gerry be in the future? Would I see Mark again, or would he take Gerry out when I was gone?

In my mind's eye I saw him balanced with his legs apart on the wildly tossing Hobie Cat as he sailed recklessly close to the *Black Tern,* and I knew that more than anything else in the world I wanted to believe what he had told me this afternoon on the boat, just before the Coast Guard cutter arrived.

Presently Aunt Kara came upstairs with a tray and sat on the edge of the bed while I satisfied my hunger with the thick beef sandwich and glass of milk she had brought me.

"They will be here tomorrow, Gilly, dear, all of them. Your folks are bringing Gerry, who will have to make her statement to the police."

"I feel for her."

"And then," Aunt Kara said gently, "you can both tell us your stories."

I knew she was dying to question me, and I was grateful to her for realizing I was too exhausted to talk. She patted my shoulder, took away the tray, and left me to get some much-needed rest.

* * *

When Gerry got out of the car I saw that she was not wearing the yellow knit dress. Mine was hanging in the closet upstairs. I had taken it out but had been unable to put it on. I was not sure I would wear it again. Gerry looked subdued. Detective O'Brien got out of a car parked behind my dad's and followed them up the walk.

I watched them from a bay window in the living room, and then flew down the stairs to meet them in the foyer.

"Moth-er-r-r!" I heard Gerry cry as she rushed into Aunt Kara's arms.

"Are we back to that?" Aunt Kara said, with a catch in her laugh.

"Do you mind?"

"Call me anything you like, honey!" Aunt Kara said, her voice buried in Gerry's hair for a moment before she released her to Uncle Justin.

My dad grinned at me and took both me and Mom in a bear hug.

Gerry finally broke away from her parents and looked at me. "I'm sorry, Gilly."

I shrugged. "Sorry" was inadequate.

Detective O'Brien asked us if we could sit down for a moment, and we all trooped upstairs to the living room and made ourselves comfortable. He remained standing while he told us Herbert Pound had been charged with the hired murder of his wife.

"We will probably add kidnapping and attempted assault with intent to murder to that. That means, of course, that you girls

149

will both be called as witnesses," he said, "along with Mark Dolan."

"There goes your trip to Europe, Gerry," Uncle Justin said.

Detective O'Brien observed mildly, "The trial won't come up for months, Mr. Partridge, the calendar is so crowded. It should be possible for you to get permission to leave the jurisdiction of the court for a short time."

"Can you tell us what happened the day Mrs. Pound died?" my father asked him.

"We are still investigating that, Mr. Topper, but I can tell you that Herbert Pound's wife was threatening to divorce him," Detective O'Brien said, "and the settlement was going to expose his embezzlement."

Aunt Kara sat up. "Lisa never mentioned a divorce to me!"

Mr. O'Brien glanced at her. "She had spoken to a lawyer who says Herbert Pound did not want a divorce. It was her money, you see. Mrs. Pound and her sister inherited the family business, and they had left the management pretty much to Herbert. A divorce suit would mean a careful audit of his books, and this was something he couldn't face. The charges against him will say he hired a killer, then took his wife out on his boat and set her up as a target."

The detective's matter-of-fact recital made it seem even more horrible.

"Poor Lisa!" Aunt Kara exclaimed. "I just can't believe it — a man like Herb Pound! Can you, Justin?"

"I certainly had no idea Herb was capable of such a thing. But what did Gerry have to do with this?"

Detective O'Brien looked at my twin. "Do you want to tell them, Gerry?"

Gerry looked at Kara and Justin. "Do you remember the night after it happened, when he was here?" she asked them. "And people kept dropping in, and everyone was so sorry for him, and he excused himself and left the living room? Well, I went up to my room, and there he was, using my private line to make a phone call!

"When I walked in, he was saying, 'Not to worry. The chief of police himself told me some kid was shooting at a gull.' I stopped in the doorway, thinking I had misunderstood. I couldn't believe what I was hearing. Then he said, 'Okay, okay! I've got the cash, but we can't be seen together. Be at the drop at midnight.' He hung up and turned around, and there I was."

She shivered. There were hollows under her eyes I had not noticed before. "I said, 'What are you doing in my room?' and he said, 'I wanted a little privacy, Gerry, but I didn't have it, did I?' It was the way he said it, so cold. It just popped out. I said, '*You* did it!'"

Gerry hugged herself. "His eyes! They wiped me out."

I knew the look. I had seen it aboard the *Black Tern*.

Gerry was going on. "'If you say that

again,' he told me, 'to me or anyone else, the same thing could happen to Kara. Or Justin. Or your brother. Remember that.'" Gerry's voice was trembling as she finished. "Then he just walked by me and down the stairs. I was petrified. I didn't say anything, to anybody! But then the phone calls began coming, on my private line. And I — I just didn't know what to do."

"Is that why you begged us to take you to Europe this summer?" Uncle Justin asked her.

Gerry nodded. "I thought if we planned a trip — I didn't care where we went, really. I — I just had to get away."

"And that's when you learned you had a twin," I said. "How convenient!" My tone was hard, and six people looked at me in surprise.

"Gilly, I feel terrible about it — "

Detective O'Brien interrupted Gerry. "Well, I'll be in touch, Mr. Partridge," he said, and Uncle Justin walked with him down to the foyer.

I stood up and ran up the stairs to Gerry's third-floor bedroom. She felt terrible? I felt terrible. There was a hard stone where my stomach should have been.

The morning fog had burned off, and the water was a sparkling blue beyond the wharf. I stood at the window, looking out at the view I would not be seeing anymore. I could see a tiny bit of the black hull of the *Balclutha* and I remembered Mark showing me the collection of painted figureheads, all women, that had sailed on the bowsprits of old vessels.

Already the bay was dotted with sails, most of them white, with here and there a bright-colored one marking a Hobie Cat like Mark's. It came to my mind that if Gerry had not persuaded me to change places with her, I might never have come to know Mark Dolan. Would he have searched me out in my valley town after that accidental kiss he said was so special? Or would it have been just a poignant memory for each of us, never to be repeated?

I heard Gerry's light step on the stair and turned to face the open door. She came in dispiritedly and sank down on the nearest bed. "I know how you feel, Gilly, but you can't feel as awful as I do. I couldn't sleep last night thinking you might have been killed and it would have been all my fault."

I didn't answer her.

"I was in such a blue funk," she admitted, "that I would have done anything to get away. But, Gilly, I didn't intend to put you in danger, truly. I was so frightened of Herb Pound that I didn't really believe you could fool *him* for long. I guess I was too scared to think straight because it didn't occur to me that when he found out he would just assume you knew what I knew."

When I still did not speak, she said in a small voice, "You're stronger than I am, Gilly. You stood up to Herb Pound, and I caved in and ran."

"I stood up to him, all right," I muttered.

"I threatened to call the police and nearly cost both of us our lives."

But I remembered Sheilah asking, *Who's dominant? Was I really the dominant twin, after all?* I studied Gerry. She sat there, bowed over, her hair falling over her forehead, looking so much like me in my depressed moments that I knew exactly how miserable and remorseful she felt.

Two parts of the same seed.

"You knew what Herb Pound had done, and I didn't," I told her, feeling my way. "Who knows what I would have done in your place?"

"Justin said I should have told him immediately. But I was just too terrified."

"You were frightened for them, Gerry, and not for yourself," I said, slowly. "That makes a difference."

She laughed, a little choked sound. "Oh, I was afraid for me, too!" But she looked up at me gratefully, and the hard stone inside me began to dissolve. I felt more buoyant already. Once again we were tacitly sharing our emotions.

We heard the front knocker faintly, and then Aunt Kara was calling up the stairs, "Mark is here to see you, Gilly."

I did not move.

Gerry's look turned speculative. "So that's the way it is. Is it serious?"

"I think so. Do you mind?"

She shook her head. "No, I'm happy for you, Gilly. I like Mark a lot."

"But you like Ryan better?"

"No-o-o." Suddenly she laughed. "But I like him a lot, too. I'm not ready to be serious yet."

I nodded, understanding perfectly. I left the window and she stood up. We hugged each other. Gerry said, "I'm glad I found you, Gilly."

"So am I."

"Let's spend as much time together as we can. Maybe Dad will ask you to go to Europe with us when this is all over. Would you go?"

"Would I!"

"It would be fun, wouldn't it? You know, Gilly, this is not such a bad arrangement, is it? The way things have worked out? Of course, we never would have found each other if I hadn't needed a passport! But now they can't keep us apart. And it just means we'll have four parents instead of two."

"I'm not sure I can cope with four," I said.

Gerry laughed. "I'm not sure *I* can cope with two!"

"But we've got each other now."

We hugged again. Then I ran down the stairs to Mark.